T0333596

Barcelona

Barcelona

MARY
COSTELLO

CANONGATE

First published in Great Britain in 2024 by Canongate Books Ltd,
14 High Street, Edinburgh EH1 1TE

canongate.co.uk

2

Versions of some of these stories have been published as follows: 'The Choc-Ice
Woman' appeared in the *New Yorker*, 'Assignation' was broadcast on RTÉ, 'My Little
Pyromaniac' appeared in *The Long Gaze Back* (New Island Books), '*Deus Absconditus*'
appeared in the *Irish Times*, 'Barcelona' appeared in *Town and Country: New Irish Short Stories*
(Faber), 'The Hitchhiker' appeared in *Silver Threads of Hope* (New Island Books).

Excerpt from 'Little Viennese Waltz', taken from *Poet in New York* by Federico García
Lorca. Copyright © Federico García Lorca. Published by Penguin Classics. Reprinted
by permission of Penguin Books Ltd.

The author received financial support from the Arts Council of Ireland
in the creation of this work.

British Library Cataloguing-in-Publication Data
A catalogue record for this book is available on
request from the British Library

ISBN 978 1 80530 183 7
Export ISBN 978 1 80530 184 4

Typeset in Centaur MT by Palimpsest Book Production Ltd,
Falkirk, Stirlingshire

Printed and bound by CPI Group (UK) Ltd, Croydon CR0 4YY

In memory of my father
Thomas Costello
1928–2004

Contents

Beyond the boards the forest begins.

Franz Kafka, 'A Report to an Academy'

Barcelona

They had not long arrived in the city. They had driven all day on the motorway, over high bridges and around wide sweeping bends, with cars speeding past and trucks bearing down on them and only a low metal guard shielding them from the ravines below. The drive had terrified Catherine. She had kept her head down. David had not seemed to notice, or hear her, when she asked if they could please get off the motorway.

Their hotel was on a narrow street off the Ramblas where Picasso had once lived over a jewellery shop. They walked out into the bright shopping streets, and parted company for a while. Catherine strolled around, in and out of expensive boutiques with gleaming tiled floors and semi-bare rails. Through La Boqueria, the covered market with its trays of tongues and hanging hams. Now and then she stood before a shopfront or a billboard – the colours of Spain, of Miró, everywhere. The afternoon sun beat down. Once, she caught sight of David up ahead and ducked into a shop. She found a café down a side street and sat outside with coffee and a cigarette. Sometimes she thought she could live on cigarettes alone, silently, deeply inhaling, letting thoughts gather, coalesce, then purge themselves in the exhalation.

Later, together, they walked in the shade of the plane trees on the Ramblas. The birds, locked up for siesta, were silent. Rabbits and tortoises too. Canarios €14. Pico de Coral €20. Isabellas €25. Arrival in a new city often reminded Catherine of her youth, the pining for home she would feel on Sunday nights as her bus approached the city and the orange lights up ahead bled into the horizon. Now her mind was crowded by details of the day, the drive, the week ahead. It was their fourth anniversary, and this trip, this city, had been David's choice. She knew he wanted it to matter, to mean something to them afterwards. Setting out that morning, she had brought up Lorca, whose poems she had taken with her.

'He was from Granada, or near Granada,' she said. She looked out the window at the orange groves, the scorched headlands, the limpid day. 'He was murdered by the Fascists in the thirties. It's still a sensitive issue here.'

David shrugged. Before they joined the motorway she took out the poems. *In the dark wake of your footsteps, my love, my love.*

'They never found his grave,' she said. *See how the hyacinths line my banks! I will leave my mouth between your legs, my soul in photographs and lilies.*

She would have preferred Granada. She would have liked to find the mountain road near Alfacar where Lorca was shot and buried. 'He was chasing *duende*,' she said. 'That's what he was after.' She looked at David. 'Do you know what *duende* is?'

He shook his head. 'No. Tell me. What's *duende*?'

She was surprised to find herself doing this, making him feel less, under par. He was proud, accomplished in his own field – the law – and generally peaceable. She was in a strange mood. Lately she found herself growing dismissive, impatient, employing at times a withering attitude towards him.

'It means soul,' she said. 'The dark cry of the soul, the terrible sadness that seizes the flamenco singer.' He was staring straight ahead. 'The grief and hardship in her voice,' she said.

She watched him search for a reply, for some comparison he might offer. The singer falls into a trance, he might say, like in *sean-nós*, or old women's keening. *Yes*, she'd say. The kind that goes to the marrow, he'd say. *Yes. Yes.* She waited, but he offered nothing. 'She is haunted by love,' she continued. 'Deranged by love, and death too. There's always death.'

They were approaching the motorway then. She found her mind veering off into an imagined conversation. After a while she turned to him. 'Why do couples always make love – desperate frantic love – after a big row?' she asked.

They wandered around the port and along narrow streets, stopping now and then to gaze up at the buildings. A spaniel came out of a courtyard and sat on the footpath, calmly looking at her. They walked for a long time. They did not know where they were going. In a doorway a teenage boy stirred and looked up at her with deep-set, familiar-looking eyes and she was filled with a mild panic that he might speak to her, say her name even.

They returned by different streets and came upon a procession of altar boys carrying a cross and banners, and priests wearing robes and pointed hats like the Ku Klux Klan. At the rear, a brass band played, and uniformed young men rode on horseback, and she thought there was something haughty and triumphalist in their bearing, something in their perfectly sculpted features and flawless olive skin – the whole spectacle, in fact – that chilled her. David smiled and raised his eyebrows as if to say, *Okay? Enjoying this?* He took out his map. 'That used to be a bullring,' he said, pointing across the street. 'There's one still in use not far from here. We should go, before they outlaw it.'

Later, in a restaurant, he brought up the bullfight again. 'Seriously, we should go. There's one on Sunday.' She shrugged. She thought it was a test. They were drinking Rioja. The restaurant was crowded, buzzing with talk. He had ordered *codorniz*, quail, and when the waiter arrived and put down his plate, the scrawny little bird toppled over. Just then a woman at the next table let out a sharp laugh that startled Catherine. David righted the carcass and tapped on the breast bone. He peeled back the skin and teased a morsel of moist dark meat from the rib cage and raised it to his lips. She turned away. A terrible piercing loneliness entered her. A scene from a book, from years ago, surfaced. *Justine.*

There were lovers – maybe a love triangle – and hazy bedroom scenes, and beyond the window the heat and bustle of a North African city. A camel collapsed from exhaustion on the street outside, and men with axes came and hacked off its limbs and carved up its flesh while it was still alive. What she remembered, especially, was the pained, puzzled look in the camel's eyes, and the eyes moving as its limbs were cut off. The eyes still moving as the head was hacked off.

The woman at the next table laughed again, and Catherine looked at David. She began to picture the walk back to the hotel, the bedroom, their nakedness. She had had the feeling, setting out that morning, of going someplace, and now she had ended up somewhere else, somewhere that made her more homesick than ever.

David was smiling, holding out a small red box. Inside were earrings, amethyst.

She frowned. 'I didn't get you anything.'

'I don't want anything.'

She began to remove the earrings she was wearing, and put on the new ones. He sat, quietly regarding her. He would soon want children. When she tried to picture a child, it was her sister's child that always came to mind. Amy. A beautiful, pale, dark-haired little girl. Radiant with innocence. Catherine felt a strange closeness to this child that she did not feel towards the other children in the family. As if she saw Amy as she might have once been herself – a clean slate, as yet unblemished by the world – and had singled her out for saving.

She fingered the earrings. She looked at the couple at the next table. When we are young, she thought, we have enormous hope, we expect that someone – a man bearing love and mystery and new ideas – will come and help reveal us to ourselves. She looked at David's waiting face. He was no longer mysterious to her. She watched him talking sometimes, eating and drinking with gusto, bouncing through life on the solid ground beneath him, and she was struck by the distance that exists between people. How everything, the details of everyone's hidden life, far exceeds anything we can possibly imagine. And how, for brief periods, one can live at a different pitch, an extreme pitch, and then, when it has passed, return to the middle way again. Without anyone else ever knowing. No one bound her to secrecy, and she thought now that people do this – *she* did this, she kept secrets – so that they can re-imagine their lives when lived life is not enough.

On the way back to the hotel he took her hand and she walked blindly beside him. She would have liked to say something about the religious procession, the boy in the doorway, the drive that morning, them – their union. She thought there was a thread of messages on the streets, maybe even in their footsteps and in the tides of their silence, to be unriddled, but she knew that to voice such a thought would make her sound cold and remote, signal a drift in her.

In the hotel room David switched on the TV and flicked through the channels. Then he patted the bed and said 'Come here,' in a warm voice. She came and sat on the bed.

He put his hand on her shoulder, and she felt its lovely weight and closed her eyes for a few seconds. 'Are you tired?' he asked. She shook her head. He began to kiss her neck. 'Let's watch something,' he whispered.

He stopped kissing her and surfed the pay-to-view channels and then paused. A couple were having vigorous sex against a wall, the man driving hard and fast into the woman. Then the scene froze, and the menu appeared on the sidebar. David leaned towards the keyboard. He had always been keen to use porn. Everyone does, he said, and she supposed he was right, but it always left her feeling empty, and a little sickly, as if their lovemaking had been communal and he had shared her and her private raptures with others. She watched him type in their room details. Certain remote memories had a way of returning unexpectedly and, as he tapped the keys, she began to remember a night out from a time before they were married. She had not known David for long and they were in a late-night bar with two of his friends. There was a DJ and a small dance floor, and footage from old black-and-white movies was being projected up on the wall behind Catherine – clips of Laurel and Hardy, Charlie Chaplin, a flapper in a beaded dress doing the Charleston. Then, suddenly, one of David's friends laughed, and Catherine glanced back at the wall. The Charleston girl had stripped down to her bra and knickers and was doing a kind of belly dance, wriggling her ample hips and jiggling her breasts, her nipples covered in little tasseled cones. Then she turned around and bent over, exposing her backside in cut-away knickers. Catherine looked away. David gave a little whoop, then leaned in and said something to his friend. When they laughed – a low, secretive laugh – Catherine felt her heart sink. She looked into her drink. If she were a different woman she would have got up and left, but even then David had become the hub of her life, the one to prevent the drift. The friend laughed again, a guffaw this time, and David turned away to conceal his own contorted face. When she looked up the dancer was still there and, instead of knickers, a little triangular flap – a snatch or scrap of animal pelt – hung over her genitalia, attached to a thin band around her hips. She wriggled and shook and the little flap, as if part of her, wriggled and shook too, and lifted, and something struck at the heart of Catherine and she burned with shame, as if she herself were up on the wall, naked, with the little female flap flapping and hopping and lifting, and David and his friends standing there, convulsed with laughter.

He moved the cursor over the menu and clicked. Two naked girls with enormous, pumped-up breasts appeared, writhing on the screen. Catherine turned to say something but then his phone bleeped and her gaze drifted off and came to rest on the novel on the bedside table. She felt a sudden longing to return to it. To the promise of solitude, private and illicit, that it held. To the strange gaunt creature at its heart: a silent, disfigured man pushing his mother out of the city in a makeshift wheelbarrow, and then, after her death, wandering the desert, surviving on almost nothing, his mind growing emptier by the day. She had found herself worrying for him, as if he were real and in her life.

David moved up on the bed, propped himself up on the pillow, and then tugged at Catherine to join him. The TV scene changed, and a man and woman entered a ship's cabin and began kissing and clawing and tearing each other's clothes off, then panting and moaning exaggeratedly. Catherine read the subtitles, single inane words, and remained unstirred. The moaning and limb-thrashing grew louder, more phoney. She felt David grow impatient. He switched channels, began to surf for a different film. She got up and stood at the window, and he did not try to stop her. The memory of the motorway returned, the great shadows that closed over them, the monstrous trucks thundering past as they all careered downhill. In a second, everything could end. She had closed her eyes, tried not to envisage the plunge, the fall into the gorge, and when she could no longer bear it she threw off her seatbelt and climbed into the back and lay face down and motion sick for the rest of the journey.

She turned towards him now. 'I got a fright last night,' she said. 'I woke up in the middle of the night, choking.'

He threw her a glance and made a face. 'What?'

'It was a kind of nightmare. You didn't hear me?'

He shook his head, then lowered the volume. 'Why didn't you wake me?'

'It was you who was choking me.'

He hit the mute button. 'What are you talking about?'

'It was . . . a half-dream, half-real. I thought I was at home sleeping in our bed and you crept in to get something and you whispered, "Shh, go back to sleep." And then there was a thumb pressing down on my Adam's apple – hard, really hard – and I couldn't breathe and in a second the pressure surged up inside my chest – and I knew I was going to burst and my heart was going to break into pieces . . . and I said, "David, David, stop." I said it urgently, but in a nice voice too, because I knew you didn't mean it, you hardly knew you were doing it . . . I had to wake myself up to save myself. I knew I was only a second away from dying.'

She turned away. She could feel his eyes still on her.

'Why are you telling me this? What does it mean?'

'I don't know . . . Maybe you've silenced me.' She half smiled.

Then, after a moment, 'Do you remember, once, I told you about a boyfriend I had when I was nineteen?'

He shook his head.

'I did, I told you. His name was Liam.'

'The animal boy,' David said flatly. 'What about him?'

'I kept him a secret from everyone. I didn't tell you that.' David raised his eyebrows. 'It wasn't difficult,' she said. 'I had my own bedsit. He used to sleep late, watch TV while I was at lectures, smoke dope sometimes . . . He never knew his father. There was just him and his mother growing up, and sometimes foster homes.'

'What made you think of him now, tonight?'

'I don't know. The restaurant . . . The quail, maybe.'

'*Jesus Christ.*'

'Did I tell you how I met him? Maybe I did. He was giving out leaflets at the entrance to St Stephen's Green – with pictures of awful animal experiments – you know,

10

monkeys with their heads drilled open without anaesthetic, mutilated kittens, circus animals . . . And the word *vivisectionist*—'

'Jesus, Catherine,' he groaned. 'Not this old hobby-horse.'

'I remember seeing that word and thinking it was a bit like *abortionist* . . . Do you know what he told me one night? He said he was happy only once ever in his child-hood. It was a summer's evening and he and his mother were sitting in her flat as dusk fell. Just the two of them, hardly speaking . . . with the light fading, and the sound of kids playing drifting up from the yard below.'

She looked at David. 'He saw it all, you know – the abattoirs, the transport trucks, the slaughter. It tormented him – he saw it everywhere, the annihilation, the—'

'Oh, *please*, Catherine, not again! Do *not* equate the life of a cow with the life of a human being. Six million human beings.'

The sound of muffled voices carried from the next room. She was aware of naked limbs moving on the screen. 'When I was small,' she said, 'I used to hear my father getting up in the dark on winter mornings and going out and loading up cattle for the factory. He had reared them, you know, he'd looked after them every day. They walked meekly up the ramp onto the trailer for him.'

David swung his legs out and sat on the edge of the bed. 'They didn't know,' he said. 'They're not capable of compre-hending any of that.'

'They're capable of suffering.'

They looked at each other. He would always outwit her

with words, with logic. Then his shoulders seemed to slump. '*He* put all that into you, didn't he?' he said, sadly. 'All that animal business.'

She turned away. Suddenly she felt far from home. She thought of her rooms, her chair by the window, her little garden.

'He used to steal from me,' she said. 'Just little things – CDs, gift vouchers – to get money for dope. I didn't say anything . . . I couldn't.' She shook her head. 'At least when he was stoned – at least then, I thought – he might forget, he might get some peace.'

She had been incapable of tearing herself away from Liam. She had felt his silence as a kind of deprivation. And yet she almost wished to return to those times, to the fidelity of being she had felt then, the streaming across into each other, the mornings spent in bed when a thought that might have been his became hers.

David's chest was rising and falling rapidly. Suddenly he flared up. 'You were a mug, Catherine, that's what you were – a mug.'

The sound of thumping music floated up from a bar and faintly vibrated in her. She thought of the tourists on the Ramblas, the birds in their cages, wings twitching from thwarted flight.

'What happened?' David asked, in a quieter voice. 'You dumped him, I hope.'

'No. He just stopped turning up. I think he was ashamed. I searched the city for him, knocked on doors until I found his mother's flat – she was sitting in a dark room watching

TV. I'd hoped that he had run away – on the UK news sometimes I'd see protesters outside animal-testing laboratories and search for his face in the line . . .

'Eventually I went back to my old life, my old friends. And then, ages later, I got a call from his mother's neighbour. A builder had found him in a narrow gap between two buildings at the back of Capel Street, badly decomposed. He'd been missing for nearly two years. He must have climbed up there one night when he was drunk or stoned, and fallen off. Or maybe he jumped.'

She used to imagine him drifting in and out of consciousness, the footfall of strangers on the far side of the wall. His brain winding down after death. Everything deeply and terribly wrong. She went to her parents' house in the country for a while, and lay on her old bed in the evenings, conjuring up his final hour. It was always night-time and he would stop on the street, tilt his head as if discerning a cry above the din of traffic, then glance up and catch a glimpse, an apparition – of what? A cat perched on the roof's edge, or a man – himself, his own form – silhouetted against the sky? And then his footsteps running around to the back lane and the vertiginous climb until he could go no further and he stood on the roof, eyes drilling the dark as if trying to pierce the secret of what he might become, and something at his centre – his will, his life-force – beginning to silently implode.

'I had this thought one night,' she said. 'This notion—' She hesitated, uncertain. 'It struck me that he had done it . . . intentionally. That he had sacrificed himself for the animals.

Maybe he thought they'd know – somehow they would know, and be consoled.' She looked at her husband's face. 'You have to understand,' she whispered. 'He changed my heart.'

They were silent for a long time. All day she had been waiting for something to deliver her, wanting the day to end gently.

'Tell me something,' David said then. 'Imagine, imagine there's a fire, and you can save only one thing – me or your dog. Who would you save?'

'David . . . please.' She began to cry. 'You're being silly now.'

'I'm serious! Just picture it. Who would you save?'

The image of her beloved dog, Captain, near the end of his life, appeared before her, raising his head, his misty eyes, rising on his stiff old bones to come to her when she entered the house. She thought of a fire, and Captain running through the rooms. And David.

'Answer me. In a fire, who would you save?' His eyes were penetrating her.

'I'd save you both,' she whispered.

'Not allowed! You know the rules. *Choose.*'

She took a step away from the window but there was nowhere to go. She thought of her father's cattle locked in the shed the night before their journey, sensing something – the approach of an awful dawn. *Yes, a holocaust,* she wanted to say. And we are all complicit. And I am complicit too – because I say nothing, I do nothing. But she could not say it. What words would she use? How could she say that

14

when she saw her father walking into his barn in springtime, with a tin of rat poison in his hand, that a vision of such catastrophic, such apocalyptic proportion loomed before her – of rats, legions of rats, gasping, dragging their swollen bellies on the ground? Crazed, running rats. Females shedding the contents of their wombs on the concrete floor. How could she say such things? How could she ask if the terror of rats is less than that of any other species?

'I cannot help it,' she said. 'It's what I see. And it's getting worse – I see it everywhere. In sheds, in fields . . . their waiting. And at Christmas when your mother lifts the turkey out of the oven and bastes it and prods it with a skewer till the juices run clear, I think of her, and my own mother too – good women, full of human kindness – as executioners. And everyone around the table feasting on this poor corpse – and Amy too, sweet Amy, growing more tainted and tarnished with each bite – and all I feel is shame, and I sit there thinking, "Are they all mad? Has the world gone mad? Or am I the mad one?" Am I, David?'

He was staring with wide-open eyes. For a second, she glimpsed a hint of mercy in them. But then a look of bafflement, or dread, began to take hold. She turned away and felt herself sway. She was almost dreaming now, with everything swimming before her. David was right – Liam had put this into her. He had left her afflicted. She saw him again on the roof that night, hardly a body at all, his gaze cast down for a long time, but then his senses slowly sharpening and heightening until every sound reached him distinctly, and he became alert to something – a dawning, a dizzying realisation that he was coming into something that might never again be his — a slowly turning earth, the opening of a vision, a vista, a promised land — the face of a father, a beautiful serene mother, a vast plain with all the beasts of the earth, wild and tame, assembled there, and in the air a note, a song, the sated sound of immortal longing rising from the tongues of birds and beasts and inanimate things. She closed her eyes and became momentarily free. She had the feeling of being there on the plain with him, called to follow, suffused in a beautiful phosphorescent light.

After a time she stirred and turned her head. David was sitting in a chair now — she had not felt him move. On the TV a man was silently rearing up on a woman, his face twisted in ecstasy. David was leaning forward, staring into a corner with desolate eyes. He put his head in his hands. At the sight of him something in her shifted. She began to perceive the damage she had done. She crossed the room and put her arms around him. She kissed the top of his head. She lifted his right hand and pressed it to her breast, urging him, willing him to take hold, and for a moment she felt a give, a fleeting submission, in him. But then, as soon as she let his hand go, it fell away and he let it fall, and it swung for a moment and then hung by his side, pale and limp and indifferent.

Deus Absconditus

It is Martin's first time on the Eurostar. He happens to be in London, and is taking this opportunity to meet his son, John, who is over from the US for a science conference in Paris. The train sweeps past the back gardens and industrial estates of Greater London. Out in the country, a light rain begins to fall. He opens his book, but cannot concentrate. A bluebottle lands on the bright-green sleeve of a young man sitting diagonally across from him. He studies the bluebottle, the casual landings and take-offs. The young man has a pale impassive face, and mild blue eyes. Martin thinks he is not looking at anyone or anything, but far off inside himself. Then, slowly, the man's eyes begin to fill with tears. When he blinks they fall on his face, his hands. Martin looks away. They are speeding through Kent, over the chalky earth. He is waiting for the plunge underground. He remembers the giant drilling machines that bored under the seafloor from either side years ago, and met in the middle. He looks back at the young man and he is drawn in, confounded. Who did this to you? he thinks.

17

He grows anxious, waiting for the plunge. He has a fear of enclosed spaces, suffocation. A polo-neck jumper pulled over his head as a child; the slide into an MRI scanner last year; the Aillwee Caves, years ago, when Mona and the boys scrambled ahead of him into the long, low passageways. He feels a shift, a drop in speed, and there follows a gradual descent. An eerie silence falls on the carriage. Then the lights come on. From the tunnel walls there is no way of knowing where land ends and sea begins. He wonders what psychic perturbations are induced in man as he descends into these subterranean depths, the fish above his head, him so long ashore. Mona would dismiss such thoughts with a click of her tongue. It would be better if you said your prayers, she would say. She is in Spain for a week with members of Galway Bridge Club. Since retirement, he and Mona measure out their time in holidays and weekend breaks, often taken separately. He struggles to come up with destinations of his own. This week he visited his sister in London. Travel heightens the senses, makes small, easily forgotten details more acute, significant, imperishable. Travel makes of home a wound that accompanies him everywhere.

He gets up and goes to the toilet. He cannot pee. The undercarriage rattles and clangs, and he is thrown against the side of the tiny compartment. He steadies himself, but still his urethra will not relax and release the contents of his bladder.

On his way back to his seat, the tilt of a woman's face reminds him of Mona and he feels a little leap of hope. And then, as he takes his seat, they are suddenly in daylight again, passing vast fields, wind farms, villages with red roofs and church spires, being swept rapidly eastwards, as if everything lies there. He turns his head by degrees. In the distance, a line of poplars. The words 'Balm of Gilead' spring to mind. It is a variety of poplar. The nursing home in Athlone where his mother died was called Balm of Gilead. The name comes from the Old Testament. *Is there no balm in Gilead? Is there no physician there? Why then is there no healing for the wounds of my people?*

At Gare du Nord he follows the signs for the RER B. He has planned everything meticulously, left nothing to chance. On the platform he is buoyed up – he likes this feeling of being a lone traveller. He will sit at an outdoor café and read his novel. He might smoke a cigarette. He would like to get away from the man he is at home.

He gets off at Luxembourg and climbs into the sunny street and walks to his hotel on rue Pascal. In a matter of hours, he will see his son. He will, again, be with his own kin, his own blood. For a few moments, he is extraordinarily happy.

Later, with his map, he makes his way along the streets towards the Panthéon. He passes a homeless man asleep on a grille, warm air wafting up from the Métro. He remembers the rickety little trains from previous visits, tumbling up hill and down dale through the underground, careering dangerously around bends, screeching into stations. He walks with his head down, counting his footsteps, abstractedly keeping their beat until he enters, in his mind's eye, the labyrinthine tunnels below, the fragile honeycomb foundations of the city, and, caught between worlds, he experiences a brief vertiginous wobble, a misstep, so that he has to stop, put a hand on a wall, find his bearings again.

He passes a church, fine stone buildings. He finds the square and the café that Hemingway frequented, and sits outside, and orders lunch. He looks around. Paris is vain, he thinks, too beautiful, too pleased with itself. He watches people crossing the cobbles and thinks of home, the sea close by, the small fields and tender landscape surrounding the city. He checks his watch and remembers John, just a few streets away now, at the Sorbonne. He would like to see more of his first-born son. The trip to London was mostly a pretext to come here and see John.

Afterwards, he returns along the same streets, past the Panthéon and rue Soufflot. He enters the Luxembourg Gardens. The place is teeming with people, walking in the shade of trees, sitting in chairs by the fountain. He makes his way along the central axis and finds a seat beside a large wooden planter in which a tree grows. At the fountain, children are pushing little sailboats out onto the water with sticks. He used to make the boys swim all year round at Salthill. He made them dive from the diving board into the freezing water, to toughen them up. He turns his head. A wood pigeon has landed on the rim of the planter beside him. In the sun its plumage is beautiful, luminous. As he watches, it bows its head and raises its tail and defecates into the planter. He looks around to see if anyone else has noticed. He thinks of this private act and the multitude of private acts unfolding in the tumult around him. Each act, each object and being in its own destiny; the pigeon in his too. The *corpus mysticum* that contains everything, every breath ever breathed, every deed ever done.

And then, a little commotion at the fountain: a bright-red, remote-controlled motorboat has zoomed out onto the water and is whizzing around, all swagger and flash, among the sailboats. In the flurry, a sail tilts and the motorboat becomes entangled in its fabric, and is immobilised. It revs and splutters, but it is crippled, and for several minutes it is towed along by the sailboat, both of them tacking back and forth to the whim of the breeze, limping home. Martin smiles and turns away, but within seconds the motorboat is roaring back out on the water, teasing, taunting, looking for trouble.

Before he leaves, he wanders into the Orangerie where a photographic exhibition is running. *La Grande Guerre.* Some of the photographs are of the trenches, but most are of Paris. A dead horse lies in the middle of rue San Antoine as people go about their business. The tail is limp in the dust, the bowels evacuated, the vulva exposed. He stands before her, shamed. Further along, a wedding, women in munitions factories, a dead soldier beside a crater. The ruins of Ypres: silent souls among the asphodels.

At six-thirty John comes to his hotel, and they embrace awkwardly in the foyer. This gesture the only exterior equivalent of his heart's motion that is permitted. John is tanned, beginning to grey at the temples. They walk towards the river. Martin asks after Rachel and the children, John after his mother and brothers. They turn left and wander along Boulevard Saint-Germain. The traffic is louder here so they cannot easily talk. Occasionally, their arms touch. They find a small bistro off the boulevard and take a table inside, grateful for the waiter's approach, and for the wine. John tells him there was an electrical storm over Paris last night. Very dramatic, he says — forks of lightning, the full acoustics of thunder, the sky lit up in apocalyptic fashion.

His accent, after twenty years away, is more American, making Martin feel self-conscious, embarrassed almost, about his own. 'How's the conference going?' he asks.

'It's going well,' John says. 'It ends tomorrow.' He will return to Boston on an evening flight. He did not present a paper this year. He is in the process of changing direction, research-wise, he says, but does not elaborate.

Sometimes Martin googles John. The articles he comes upon by his son are obscure and, it seems to him, growing more so all the time. John is a biochemist, and in the early years of his career Martin did his best to acquaint himself with the various branches and strands and developments in biochemistry, and with polymerisation, which was John's field at the time. He had been hopeful. He had read a book, *Heraclitean Fire*, the memoirs of a scientist. He had put his hand on it in a bookshop, thinking it was on Gerard Manley Hopkins. But it was the writings of a biochemist, and he had bought it, struck by the synchronicity of coming on such a book just as John was starting his post-doctorate research at MIT. There are things Martin still remembers from that book, things that surprised and uplifted him – Latin words, insights, language that was poetic. The scientist had a melancholy nature. He had a deep pity for little words when they were mistreated.

The waiter takes their order and they settle in. John pours the wine. A man at the next table raises his glass to his lips. He reminds Martin of a friend, an ex-colleague. All day long he has been fastening on faces, superimposing the features of loved ones or acquaintances onto strangers, creating a multiplicity of phantoms in an attempt – he now thinks – to keep homesickness at bay.

'How was the train ride over?' John asks.

'Good,' Martin says. 'Better than I expected.' He is about to say that he kept imagining the tunnel roof collapsing and the sea bursting in. But he holds back. He feels a weight gathering, the whole evening pressing down on him. He remembers the crying man on the train. Why had he assumed his suffering had been inflicted by others? He might have done something himself, some crime.

'And you saw Ellen in London – how is she?' John asks.

'She's good. You know Ellen – ever the revolutionary, the campaigner. Still the occasional thorn in Mother Superior's side, I suspect.'

Ellen, his sister, is a nun. Once, he had pitied her for all the life she had forsaken by taking her vows. In their youth he had argued intensely with her. But the older he gets, the more he seeks her out. Her presence, and their shared past, evoke in him feelings of peace and ease and reverie. 'She's working on another book,' he says.

'Good for her! What's this one on?'

'Women. Peace women – the Israeli women who keep vigil at the border crossings. The Quaker, Prudence Crandall. Another woman – whose name I've forgotten – who was the first US Congresswoman. Apparently she voted against going to war twice – first in 1917, and again in 1941 – she was the only one to vote against attacking Japan.'

'Wow. Ellen is amazing, at her age.' He smiles kindly. 'Auntie Nun.'

The boys gave her this name when they were small. She brought them books, exerted an influence, raised the bar. She had done the same for him when they were young. He had thought then he was destined for something unusual. But all he had been was a husband, a father, a provincial schools' inspector.

Around them, animated conversations in French, voices speaking at the same time. He looks at John. He wishes he had more common ground with him, and not this over-demanding heart. He observes other men with their sons. There is a way of being that some men have that allows them to take their sons into their lives.

Then he brightens, remembering something. When John was small, he had a gift. In an uncanny way, he knew things. He would open a drawer, or lift a cushion, and silently hand Mona the lost keys or the missing sock she was searching for. Who's that? she would ask him, pointing to the face in a photograph – an old friend or distant relative that he had never met and could not possibly have known – and he would turn his solemn little face towards her, and simply

24

say the name. Margaret. Frank. One winter's evening when the electricity was out during a storm he walked calmly out to the hall, opened the little door of the boxed-in alcove, and touched something – a loose fuse perhaps – and returned light to the whole house. Martin does not know when his powers vacated him, or if John even remembers having them. When we remove ourselves from a certain state of being, he thinks, we lose our powers. Or maybe the ordinary murk of life settles on us and cannot be rinsed away.

'She told me a story, yesterday – Ellen,' he says, 'that I hadn't known, about my mother. And her brother, the boy who died in the Civil War.'

'I didn't know Mamó lost a brother in the Civil War,' John says. He leaves down his fork.

'She was young, maybe only ten or twelve, and one of her older brothers was active – but on the anti-Treaty side. She was very attached to him, apparently – Seán was his name. Anyway there was an ambush somewhere in north Kerry, twenty miles from their home. And he was shot, and buried hurriedly in a makeshift coffin by his companions . . . Then, ten years or so later, when she was a young woman herself, she found his grave. She had the coffin dug up and brought back to the family plot – against her father's wishes, against the other brothers' wishes too. You know how it was, brother against brother, father against son. But she did it anyway – she defied her father and had him buried in the family grave.'

'Like Antigone,' John says quietly.

He nods. 'Antigone's daughter, Ellen called her.'

They are quiet for a moment. 'But that's not it,' he says, 'that's not all of it. When they dug him up and opened the coffin, there were scratch marks on the underside of the lid. He'd been buried in a hurry, because his companions were on the run.'

John is staring at him, as he had stared at Ellen yesterday. Your God must have been in hiding that day, he had wanted to say to her.

They order coffee. 'Your mother was thinking we might visit ye in September,' he says. 'She probably mentioned that in her emails, did she? I think she's anxious to see the girls. They grow up so fast.'

They had only ever seen John's children – twin girls – once. They had had the notion that, in retirement, there would be frequent trips to Boston.

John frowns. 'September might not be the best time, Dad. It looks like we'll be moving to DC. I hadn't planned on saying anything until everything is signed, but I'm expecting to take up a new job there. Rachel is already house-hunting.'

He is taken aback. 'Oh, not to worry, then. Not to worry. Sure we can go another time.' His sips his coffee. They are quiet for some moments. 'I thought you liked MIT? And Boston?'

'I do! So it was a big decision. But this is . . . well, it's an important research project.'

'What sort of project? Which university?'

'It's not at a university. It's a government job in Maryland – at the Research Institute of Chemical Defense.'

Martin finishes his coffee. He has never heard of this institute. 'Chemical defence? That sounds . . . I don't know. What does that mean? Biological weapons, germ warfare?'

He has never had reason to question the nature of John's work, though there was a moment, years ago, watching a documentary that raised questions about some biomedical study – distorted test results, rules sidestepped in the race to succeed – when he had felt a flicker of worry. The description of the research itself, too, had troubled him. He was left with the impression of organisms under duress, cell nuclei being tortured. He knows how driven, how fiercely competitive, John can be. He knows, too, how easy it is to deviate from one's path, and transgress.

'No, Dad. Nothing like that. I won't even get close. My research area is tiny, very specialised. No new plagues incubating in my Petri dish!'

He nods. All around them the buzz of talk, the clatter of plates. Out in the city, the late-evening traffic, shutters coming down, river water flowing. He sits back in his chair. He has to have faith, like any father, that he has raised a son whose actions are governed by his conscience. He lightens up. 'I suppose Homeland Security will be running a check on your mother and myself.'

'Oh, you can be sure! It's probably already well progressed!'

They talk then about John's brothers, the economy, property prices. But he is not fully attending. There is something gnawing, something more he wants from John – a pledge, a promise, some *certainty*. He summons words, but cannot form a question. Then the words slip away and his eyes come to rest on John's hands — beautiful, white, the fingers long — and as he stares a memory from years ago surges up, as clear and bright as the waters of the lake behind him on that day. He is at a mooring on Lough Corrib, readying a boat to take the boys out on the water. They are there in the background, all three of them, mucking about. Martin must have walked back towards the car to fetch something when he came upon John — who was about ten then — hunkered down among the reeds. He was cupping something in his hands. When he saw his father, he shaped a word with his lips. *Shhh*. Poised, concentrated, he opened his palms slowly to reveal a frog, pale green, tiny, unearthly still. He had a white plastic straw clasped between his fingers, and then, in one deft movement, he upended the frog and held its head tightly in one hand and, with the straw in the other, began to prod at its rear end until he found his target and shoved the straw into the frog's anus. Before Martin could fully comprehend what was happening, John was blowing into the other end of the straw and the frog's speckled belly was expanding and maybe Martin spoke or shouted — but from this distance he cannot be sure — and in an instant the frog exploded and the tiny fragments of its shattered skin and flimsy innards dropped soundlessly to the ground.

His heart is racing. He can feel the blood throbbing in his temple. He looks across the restaurant, over the heads of the other diners until, little by little, his heartbeat slows and his thoughts begin to drift. Images from the day return: the pigeon in the Luxembourg Gardens, the little sailboats, the dead soldier on the Orangerie wall. The Germans used to crawl from the trenches, he wants to say, delirious with thirst, and drink from sulphuric puddles as the shells rained down. Scorching the earth with Heraclitean fire. That scientist was holidaying in Maine in the summer of 1945, he remembers. In the early evening of 6 August he and his wife and young son went for an after-dinner walk above a shimmering bay. They met a man who told them about a new kind of bomb that had been dropped in Japan that day. The scientist had no hand in the bomb, but he got the whiff of his own mephitic smell. He had a vision of the Devil's carnival then, blood drops from Hell, the end of the essence of man.

Darkness is falling as they walk back to his hotel. 'Maybe ye'll get home for a visit next year,' he says. He can feel the parting sickness rising inside. 'Your mother would like that.' He pictures them all at the kitchen table in Galway. Morning, the sun streaming in, Mona frying the breakfast.

'Yes, hopefully. Maybe next summer . . . Or you'll be out to visit us before then.'

They say their goodbyes at the hotel entrance, and he watches John walk away. When he has disappeared, Martin turns and walks in the opposite direction. Further and further they move away from each other. He looks at each face on the street, as in a slow dream. He thinks of the scientist above the bay, sunlight flashing on water. He begins to intuit the shudder, the intimation of terror, that all of nature must have felt that day, must go on feeling, because of what lies within any moment, because of what grows and ferments in vials and cylinders and the minds of men. *I see you, John, in your white coat, mixing and measuring and dispensing, pushing elements to new limits. How do you know your phenomena are mute? How do you know your burette is not susceptible, your shy elements are not crying out, 'Enough!'?*

He walks on. Tomorrow he will cross the Channel again. In the early evening he will touch down in Dublin and drive west across the country as atoms of light leave the sky. There is a stretch of motorway beyond Loughrea where the land rises and the light is different. He always feels its approach, the bare sky above him, a gathering within him. He presses the pedal then, million-fuelled on his own air-built thoroughfare, and drives into this throng of light, this confluence of earth and sky and road, half expecting something new to be constellated.

At the Gate

After dinner, my husband says, 'Do you want to go to Kerry next week to see that writer?'

I turn and look at him. 'Coetzee,' I say. 'What made you think of that now?'

It is Sunday evening, and we have come through another weekend.

'They were talking about it on the arts show the other evening.'

'It might be sold out now.'

'Maybe, but try anyway.'

Peter has a way of relenting, of granting favours late in the day, that is designed to make me feel grateful. When I had brought up the idea of going to this writers' festival last week he had shrugged, made a face.

'Will I book a hotel,' I ask, 'if I can get one at this stage?'

'Do. Book two nights, if you can. We'll make a weekend of it.'

Over the years, we have settled into a routine: on weekdays

there is work, dinner, TV; on weekends Peter goes hiking or rock climbing, and I have the house to myself. Mostly I read. Some days, I jot down observations on what I read or on my own thoughts and states of mind, a throwback to a youthful habit of trying to make poetry from such thoughts and states of mind, trying to recover those solitary, lit-up moments in childhood when I stood under a tree or lay on my bed on a summer's evening with the sun streaming in.

We came close to having a child once. The boy, stillborn at twenty-four weeks, had been dead *in utero* for some time. His body was dun-coloured, like a clay figure or the preserved body of a child in Pompeii, and it frightened me. When I touched his chest, my finger left an indentation, like one leaves in plasticine. Technically, it – he – was considered a miscarriage, a term I find strange. Did he miscarry, or did I? And what was I, afterwards? I could hardly call myself a mother. And if I was not a mother, could he – considering he had never actually lived or been fully gestated – be called a child? The cause of his death was inconclusive, and preventing it, I was assured, was beyond my control. But the simple, unalterable facts were that a child had died, and I was the only person responsible for him. Getting those facts to reconcile in my mind proved impossible, and I interpreted Peter's silence, and his reluctance to talk about it afterwards, not only as grief, but also as blame. Are you okay? I asked him constantly. Are *we* ok? I felt vaguely grateful, vaguely indebted to him, for just being there. This gratitude was not based on nothing: he gave off an air of mild forbearance, the impression that he could be elsewhere, in the company of someone more interesting, more fertile. And maybe he could. And maybe the quiet house, the empty rooms, the arid weekends, really were my fault.

The rhythm of our marriage is steady and predictable now, but sometimes on sleepless nights I find myself panicking, waiting for a catastrophe to strike. Maybe even wanting a catastrophe, something to burn through this life, something, even, to enliven the dull record in my notebook. When I drive out the school gate on a Friday afternoon and spot a couple on the footpath or inside the park railings talking or laughing or simply holding hands, a small hope rises in me and I think this weekend, *this weekend*, things will be different, this weekend Peter and I will turn a corner and laugh heartily and be like our younger selves again. And sometimes we do; sometimes we even make love.

On Friday afternoon we nudge our way out of the city and travel south on the motorway. Peter is relaxed, generous, almost ebullient, and I am almost happy. We should do this more often, I say. It is the end of May, my favourite time of the year, the long evenings evoking childhood memories of our cattle grazing in fields with the whole summer ahead of them. I am reminded of previous journeys like this, the conversation eventually waning, and each of us drifting in thought. Or sharing a random thought, miles from home. Peter must remember those times too — the drive down through France years ago, the heat, the erotic longing, the carnality of that trip. Light pouring in courtyard windows at dawn. There are photographs of the tiny garden flat we rented in Sainte-Maxime. Breakfast outside at a little wrought-iron table. I'm wearing a pink dress. A pink dress! Once, sitting on huge sloping rocks at the end of the pier, with a blue sky above and the sea all around, I heard the jingling of masts and turned my head and saw Peter approaching along the path between the boats and I felt such intense, unbearable love for him that I knew even then was doomed.

An hour or more into the journey, Peter says, 'So, what else do I need to know about this guy? Apart from his Nobel Prize and his . . . animal thing?'

'Animals are not his only concern,' I say, 'though they are, probably, his greatest.'

When we were first together, I pressed my literary interests on Peter, desperate to establish an affinity with each other. Peter is easily my match intellectually, but his is a mathematical mind, and he appears to have little interest in what he calls made-up stories, and none at all in poetry. In all other facets of his life — in his work, in his leisure pursuits, in his knowledge of history and politics and global affairs — he appears to have acquired mastery. Anything short of mastery leaves Peter feeling compromised, vulnerable, wounded. In one field alone — literature — I surpass him; from the start, *I* was out of *his* league and, little by little, the axis of intellectual power shifted. The axis of love too. Over the years, something has slipped, and his control has diminished. I think he blames literature for the inwardness it conjures in me, and for the fact that, increasingly, he has lost access to more and more areas of my mind. In a previous era, he might have banned certain books, or forbidden me to read altogether. Peter does not mean to belittle my reading life or the writers I admire and, for all his seeming dismissal of it, something in him longs to gain admission to that world. I see the way his eyes dart about when he enters my study, how he is at war with himself, how he has to fight the urge to pick up the book I've just left down and ask, nonchalantly, what I'm reading, and in that instant I experience something of what he is suffering, and I understand his little put-downs for what they are: unconscious attempts at self-preservation, half-conscious attempts to hold back fear or mitigate loss, and they are all forgivable.

'He moved to Australia a while back,' I say, 'disillusioned with South Africa, I think, with the way the post-apartheid state was shaping up. He doesn't give many interviews, so it's hard to know for sure.' I scan my mind for appealing facts about Coetzee that will endear him to Peter. He is a man of restraint, I could say, a man of order. He hates friction, flare-ups, angry displays. He found it difficult to reprimand his children when they were small. When I think about Coetzee, I imagine a tender, otherworldly existence and, at the same time, a bleakness, a low-level pall, falls on me.

I tell Peter that Coetzee studied Maths, that he was a computer programmer with IBM in the early sixties. Peter raises his eyebrows, makes an impressed face. He too is a Maths graduate and works as a software engineer now. When we met years ago, he explained that Maths is a discipline that accounts for and manipulates objective reality and guides us through the quantum world. On the wall of his flat, he had a framed quote from Galileo. *Nature's great book is written in mathematical symbols.* In a rare, unguarded moment, he told me he was shocked as a young teenager when he came on quantum theory, shocked at the inner workings of the atom. I suspect he was once sensitive to the inner life of numbers, alert to the visionary possibility at the heart of the quantum world, mesmerised and terrified at the thought of drawing close to those forces. Coetzee, too, must have been aware of such forces, such mysteries, in his youth. They would both have known that some men came unhinged when they drew close to that heart.

'And, oh, he once tried to run as a candidate for the European Parliament.'

Peter throws me a doubtful look. 'How was that possible, if he lives in Australia?'

'Well, he was trying to stand as a member of the Dutch Animal Party — his ancestors came from the Netherlands. But of course he couldn't, because he wasn't legally resident in the EU.'

'Huh, a publicity ploy, then.'

'He doesn't do publicity. He's very private.'

As if he regrets his little spike of sarcasm and wishes to restore the mood of benevolence, he gives a soft concessionary nod.

'And he shuns meat and alcohol,' I continue.

'*Shuns?* . . . What century are we in?'

I smile. 'I came across that in a profile of him. It suits

him, because he's formal and private and . . .' I almost say 'old-fashioned', partly to endear Coetzee to Peter, but also to deflect from the meat issue. Peter still eats meat, less so than he used to and he almost never cooks it at home, but he relishes a medium-rare steak when we eat out.

His son fell to his death from a balcony when he was twenty-three, I am about to say. Instead, I say, 'He has a character called Elizabeth Costello in one of his books.'

'I know. You told me before. Some coincidence, that.'

'Did I tell you she was born the same year as my father, 1928? In Melbourne?'

Peter keeps his eyes on the road.

'Some of my father's uncles emigrated to Australia in the late 1890s,' I say.

'She's a fictional character. Just because she shares your surname doesn't mean . . . It's just a coincidence.'

Peter thinks I attach too much significance to coincidences, that I am too quick to see signs and meanings in ordinary, random events. He is thinking that now. It is a trait that irritates him. Too permeable, too suggestible, too. Even my allergy to certain smells and chemicals – perfume, cleaning products, diesel fumes which cause headaches and trigger migraines – rankles with him. Last week when he came downstairs after a shower, the scent coming off him was new and harsh and I felt the beginnings of a headache instantly.

'Is that a new shampoo?' I asked.

'Nope. Same shampoo as ever.'

'Well, something is different.'

He didn't reply.

'Is it the deodorant?' I asked.

A sudden flash of rage then. 'You are impossible to live with,' he spat, '*fucking* impossible.' Peter detests any loss of control, and afterwards suffers deep remorse for his outbursts. 'It's worse you're getting, you know. This . . . concentrating on *every little thing*. You need to stop this.'

The headache was taking hold. I could hear his voice rising, then falling, the last word ebbing away. *This . . . this . . . this . . . this . . .* Looking first into his eyes and then into his mouth, I had the odd sensation of time altering and light moving around my head, the way it does before an ocular migraine strikes. But there was no aura, no psyche-delic patterns. Then, simultaneously, a sensation, like déjà vu, but one in which I perceived everything concurrently. Present time disintegrated, and past, present and future coexisted. For a moment I had a knowledge of eternity. Not only was I aware of my own past and present and eternity and all the events therein, but the pasts, presents and eternities of others. There was no distinction between illusion and reality. I was like Hamlet, bound in a nutshell and yet king of infinite space. Afterwards, when I tried to record this sensation in my notebook, what came to mind was the narrator in that Borges story who saw the infinite Aleph — the point in space that contains everything — enclosed in a small iridescent sphere under a step of a cellar stairs. Every point in the universe was visible to him. Each object was infinite objects. He saw night and day contemporaneously, the dawn and the dusk, the sea. He saw the multitudes of America and all the ants on earth; he saw tigers, bison, groundswells, armies; he saw clusters of grapes, snow, every grain of sand in the equatorial deserts. He saw the circulation of his own blood, and in Inverness he saw the undetected cancer in the breast of a woman he would never forget. At the end, he cried with compassion for the inconceivable universe.

We get off the motorway and drive through Tipperary on the old road to Limerick. We pass lush farmland with cows grazing. It is starting to happen again, the torment I felt in my twenties that caused me to see animal suffering at every turn: in every field and farmyard, in passing livestock trucks, in circus wagons fetched up on the outskirts of towns. I breathe deeply and exhale slowly. Up ahead, a bright-green sign announces *Clodagh's Garden Centre, 2km.* How is it that the sight of certain names can strike at the heart of us? Clodagh was the little girl a few years younger than me in primary school whose father was killed crossing the road at Bunratty Castle. Her mother was pregnant with Clodagh at the time. 'Imagine,' I heard my own mother telling my aunt, 'imagine, she became a wife and a widow and a mother all in one year.' I was always aware of Clodagh hovering at the edge of the schoolyard, thin and pale and silent, nibbling her sandwich. Marked out as special, like an orphan in a novel. I never once heard her speak. I doubt if any teacher pressed her to answer a question, even to say *Anseo*. Her mother was thin and pale and quiet too. She took Clodagh onto her lap at Mass on Sundays. I imagined them at home, communicating in a language known only to them, as they waited patiently, biding their time until they'd join Clodagh's father.

We pass the garden centre on the left, a half-empty car park in front of a large glass-fronted building, behind which are surely polytunnels and rows of potted shrubs, flowers, trees. Nothing at all that might suggest a Clodagh, except maybe the after-hours feeling in the empty car park late in the evening. I wanted to be like her, part angel, part girl. Unborn when her father died, the two souls passing each other in transit. Clodagh herself died when she was twelve, after getting a belt of a sliotar playing camogie. Who on earth sent that child onto a playing field? I was in secondary school by then. In class, I thought of Lazarus, and Jesus, and now Clodagh, no ordinary human child.

I like when Peter tells me stories from his childhood, though we have exhausted his store by now. Not much to tell, he says, whenever I ask. His father was sixty when Peter was born, a strict, authoritarian man. The abiding image I have of Peter is of a worried little boy retreating to his room in an unnaturally silent household. One story from his childhood has stayed with me. He was about ten or eleven, watching an old black-and-white film starring Clint Eastwood. Clint is on horseback, on a ranch round-up or a long cattle drive out west, Peter was not sure which. At one point, the herd has to cross a swollen river and, in the chaos, a small calf gets into difficulty. Clint spots it just in time and throws a lasso around the calf's neck and pulls it to safety. Afterwards, thinking about the film, Peter had a sudden realisation: that calf is dead now, he thought; they are all dead – the calf and the cows and the horse Clint is riding – are all long gone.

I keep my eyes on the road ahead. I begin to compile a mental list of things I find amazing – no, miraculous. The growth of fingernails. The migration of birds. The collectivist social intelligence of insects. The idea of forgiveness. Years ago, my therapist suggested this exercise as a means of quelling anxiety and, occasionally, I still call on it.

'Don't you think it's miraculous that there aren't more deaths by suicide on the roads?' I ask Peter. Start with familiar things, the therapist said, start with what's right there in front of you.

Peter makes a face. 'Miraculous?'

'Yes, miraculous. The fact that we set out in our cars every day, and survive. When you think about it. Every time you sit behind the wheel, you have to have one hundred per cent trust that every driver coming towards you – barrelling towards you at a hundred kilometres an hour, like this, now – will be responsible and competent and sane.'

For months after the miscarriage, I could not drive, or cross a busy street, or walk further than the end of our cul-de-sac. I wanted only to be alone. At the sound of Peter's key in the door, my heart sank.

'Why are you saying this?' Peter asks. 'You've been driving since you were seventeen. You know well that ninety-nine per cent of drivers are responsible and competent and, yes, sane.'

'I know. But think how hazardous driving is. Look,

41

look, we're only a few feet from that car. See? One slight wobble or a moment's distraction and we plough into each other.'

I turn and look at him. Recently, I came on a magazine article about an Irish woman who had converted to Islam. She told a story about a man who went to the prophet Muhammad for advice because he no longer loved his wife. Muhammad looked at the man and said, Go home and love her. *Just love her*, he said.

'That's different to *deliberately* ploughing into someone,' Peter says. 'Which is what you said. Suicide by car is what you said.'

'No, it's not. I said isn't it a *miracle* that more people don't commit suicide by car. You know, like suicide by cop.'

Peter is not the kind to suffer sudden impulses. He can stand at the edge of a cliff without feeling gravity's pull. He can meet cars on a straight stretch of road without feeling the urge to turn the steering wheel a little and drive headlong into the next one.

'Fear of being left a vegetable, I suppose,' he says, 'might be the reason there isn't more "suicide by car", as you call it. Collateral damage to others too. Anyway, isn't suicide by car when you step out in front of an oncoming car?'

We stop off in Roscrea and refuel the car. We find a café we remember from a previous journey and Peter orders at the counter, and when he turns and comes towards me with the coffees, I see how handsomely he is ageing. His DNA is in me now. Foetal cells cross into every mother during pregnancy and mix freely with her cells, resulting in a single organism, a tiny chimera, which can persist lifelong. It is odd to think of Peter as a chimera nestling deep in my microscopic cells. His mother's and father's DNA is in me too, and the DNA of all who went before them. I am no longer me. No woman who has been pregnant is ever herself again.

Peter gets up to get himself a muffin. Across the street, a white delivery van pulls up outside a supermarket. The driver gets out, removes a tray of produce and carries it into the supermarket. In red lettering on the side of the van I read:

Carroll Meats
The Slice of Life

I reach into my handbag for my notebook, write those six words, and quickly put the notebook away again. When he returns, Peter offers me a forkful of his muffin. Blueberry, your favourite, he says, smiling. I open my mouth and he feeds me some muffin. From the corner of my eye, the van moves off. Whatever I suffer, I can trace to a single cause: the doomed lives of animals.

We hit rush-hour traffic on the ring road around Limerick and enter and exit roundabouts before finally taking the N21 for Kerry. Not far now, I think. We'll just have time to check in to the hotel and have a bite to eat before the event.

'Penny for your thoughts,' Peter says.

I smile. 'Penny for your own,' I say.

And because of his earlier benevolence and maybe even

his handsomeness, and because there in kindness in his soul, I tell him more about Coetzee.

And then I see him. We have arrived in the town and are driving along the main street.

'Jesus,' I say.

Peter brakes. 'What? What's wrong?'

'That's him,' I whisper, pointing out the window.

He is walking along the footpath towards the square. Slim, white-haired, with a neatly trimmed beard, he is wearing a light-grey zip-up jacket and grey slacks. I would know him anywhere. He is in conversation with a teenage girl. His granddaughter, maybe. He doesn't have a granddaughter. We are almost level with him. He turns and says something to the girl, and his mouth widens in a smile. I have never seen him like this, so at ease. As we pass, I duck, frightened he will see me.

The sighting has thrown me. I had not expected to see him here like this, on an ordinary Irish street in this market town at evening time, in his grey jacket and slacks. I feel slightly sick, and guilty, as if I am a voyeur. How he would loathe this intrusion, this appropriation, my pre-sumption of intimacy. I might remind him of his mother. I am not Vera, I want to say. Peter says something, but I am not listening.

We check in at the hotel reception and freshen up and then go down to the hotel bar and order food. I can barely swallow. The place is bustling; I recognise writers, journal-ists, media people. We do not belong here. Peter is silent, uncomfortable in this milieu too, and hurt and baffled by my withdrawal. I keep glancing at my watch, picturing the conference room. When I try to picture the stage on which he will stand or sit, it is not him but his creation, Elizabeth Costello, I see, old and tired and contrary, standing at a lectern in an American university. In her blue cotton frock, with her greasy hair, she is speaking to an audience of academics about the unspeakable cruelties inflicted on animals. Crimes of stupefying proportions, she tells her audience. She thinks she's losing her mind, she tells her son later, but every day she sees the evidence. Corpses, she whispers, fragments of corpses that people have bought for money and offer to her.

The conference room is huge, with three aisles converging towards a podium. We choose seats four rows from the front and watch the room filling up. Peter is unsettled. I leave my hand on his and he looks at me, as if to say, *What?*

There is a hush in the crowd as Coetzee is led in by a woman from the festival. They cross the floor and step onto the podium. Coetzee sits at a table and the woman welcomes him, adding how honoured and humbled we are to have a writer of his calibre here. She reads a brief biography, then lists his lifetime work, his awards, his extraordinary gifts.

He comes to the lectern and glances at the audience, then at his notes.

'My thanks to the organisers of the writers' festival,' he starts, 'for inviting me to County Kerry this beautiful week in spring.' His manner is formal, he is soft-spoken and polite. 'My thanks to Maura Kelly, in particular, who manages to get *so* many things done *so* efficiently and with such good humour. My thanks finally to all of you for coming to this reading when it would be so much nicer to be outdoors in the sunshine.'

He pauses and takes up some loose pages. 'I'll be reading two pieces today. The first is a story called "Nietverloren". The title, in Dutch, means "never lost" or "not lost", and it's a common name for a farm in South Africa.'

He puts on his glasses and begins to read.

The narrator of the story is recalling boyhood visits to his grandparents' farm in the Karoo. Out roaming the veld alone, the boy is puzzled by a circle of bare flat earth, marked with stones, that he thinks might be a fairy circle. Later his father tells him it is a threshing floor, where wheat was once threshed. The boy does not like the word thresh; it is too like 'thrash', to 'get a thrashing'. He does not want to be around when words like that are spoken. Threshing, he learns, was done with flails; men beat the wheat with wooden sticks to which bladders were attached – to separate the grains from the chaff. Flailing the wheat. Now, years later, the narrator of the story is back in the Karoo, driving through the empty scrubland with his wife and two American friends. Once, not long ago, farmers made a living in this region from planting crops, but now it is almost a desert where animals barely cling to life. At the end, the narrator has a sudden outburst – he is angry and bitter at the changes that have occurred in the land he loves.

Peter shifts in his seat, crosses and uncrosses his legs. I can feel the gears of his mind spinning. He does not like

Coetzee. He does not like Coetzee's voice or his manner or his story.

Coetzee reads the second piece, an excerpt from his fiction-alised memoir, *Boyhood*. Again, it is situated in the Karoo, on his uncle's farm, Volfontein, the same farm that featured in the previous story. Everything is described from the boy's point of view without emotion: the heat, the farm work, the hunting. The boy sees everything. He sees the farmhands drink from their water bottle, sheep being shorn, lambs being castrated. The food in the Karoo is delicious – the peaches, the pumpkins, the mutton, the shot venison that melts in the boy's mouth. There is nowhere on earth that means more to the boy than this farm.

I follow every word. At one point, the word desolation occurs in the text. Coetzee pronounces it *dezolation*. As he reads, he gazes out, intermittently, at the audience and when his gaze approaches, I look away in case his eyes alight on mine, in case he perceives something in them – shame that I hunger for more of his mind than is decent; guilt for the slaughtered animals of my family's farm. I look at my hands. Who is without shame, or guilt? Did he himself not pluck the wings off an insect as a child and scratch his father's favourite record? Was he not cold and heartless to a girlfriend after an abortion? Did his family not send animals to slaughter too? How are we to live with such things, to reconcile such things? When a particle of dust contains billions of atoms, how are we to reconcile anything?

He ends his reading, bows slightly, thanks the audience. My heart sinks. Why did he choose to read two such similar pieces? He remains at the lectern, rearranging his pages. The woman who introduced him – Maura – jumps up and announces that Mr Coetzee will take some questions from the audience. He turns and looks at her. Three, she says then, a little flustered, Mr Coetzee will take three questions.

The first questioner, a man, asks if Coetzee's decision to leave South Africa was political, if he was unhappy with the new South Africa. Coetzee stares out stonily, unblinkingly, at the audience.

'I think questions about . . . why one has left behind one country and . . . engaged with another are . . . more or less of the same kind of privacy as questions about why one has left one woman and engaged with another woman.'

Laughter, nervous tittering. Some clapping.

Peter turns to me. 'Really? Was that necessary?' he asks. 'Shhh.'

Another question – not a question, but a compliment on his books and his Nobel Prize. He nods graciously, thanks the woman for her kind words. This surely cannot be counted as a question. Two more to go, then. Someone will bring up the animals. Someone will bring up Elizabeth Costello, the abattoirs, the laboratories, the parched frogs. I look around for a face, a questioner, someone to ask, Are you Elizabeth Costello? Do you suffer as she suffers? How are we to make reparations to the animals?

For a moment, my heart quells and all fear and shyness leave me and I begin to compose a question. Why does Elizabeth Costello say that the reason she speaks up for animals is to save her soul? Why did you make her say that?

48

I don't believe it. I believe she'd speak out even if she knew she was going to Hell for it.

My heart is pounding loudly again. There are too many questions, too many words to entrust to my own voice. I cannot raise a hand. I am old and weary like Elizabeth herself. Then I remember that she does not exist, and there is a physical pain in my chest.

Another question about South Africa: what does Mr Coetzee think of the current state of affairs there?

Coetzee stares at the audience again. 'I believe I have already answered such a question.'

Peter is bristling. 'Why did he even come here? People paid good money to see him, and this is how he treats them?'

'Stop. Please.'

I lean forward, straining to catch every word of Coetzee's. The final question is being called. The questioner wonders why, during the apartheid era, Coetzee's own books were never banned by the South African state.

Another long silence.

Peter's chest is rising and falling rapidly. Any minute now, he will get up and walk out.

The room is holding its breath. Is it possible Coetzee didn't hear the question? Or that he considers he has already answered three? Is it possible he is insensitive to the fluctuations of feeling in the room? A murmur runs through the audience.

Peter leans in. 'This is the guy you revere? Honestly? *This* is your hero?'

Coetzee is stepping away from the lectern.

It is over. He steps down from the podium and stands there, uncertain, vulnerable. In his frail shoulders, I sense the weight of feeling he has carried around for seven decades, the toll that constantly imagining the lives of others has taken. Three people – one a well-known writer – step forward as if to speak to him, and then hang back. He is unapproachable. Maura, the festival woman, puts a hand on his arm, then beckons to someone at the back of the room. The girl who was with him on the street appears, wearing a lanyard with the festival logo around her neck. When he sees her, Coetzee lights up. She will lead him through the streets to the door of his lodgings, where he will, again, be anonymous. He will have less to say, this time, as they walk. What he desires most is to be back in the shelter of his room, to lie on the bed, close his eyes, let the evening's event recede.

The crowd moves slowly through the double doors into the corridor, and we move with them, ferried along in the heave of bodies. We close our hearts, Elizabeth Costello thinks, we refuse to imagine the lives and deaths of others. She has a vision, a plan: to build a glass abattoir in the middle of a city, an abattoir with transparent walls so that everything will be visible, the killing and butchering of animals will be visible.

The hotel foyer is buzzing. People are greeting each other, calling out to each other, holding drinks high as they manoeuvre their way through the crowd. I look towards the door. Night has fallen. The crowd is spilling out onto the front steps. All these people, talking and laughing. We stand among them for a while. I look to the door again, and crave a different kind of existence.

'Will we get a drink?' I ask.

Peter shakes his head. His mood is dark. 'I'm tired. It's been a long day.'

My stomach lurches. It is not yet ten o'clock. But Peter is already moving towards the wide curving staircase. I look around, helpless. What is it I want? To be part of this crowd, to talk about books, about Coetzee? But with whom? These people are strangers to me.

At the end of her novel, Elizabeth Costello is standing at the gate to the afterlife, or to whatever comes next. Before she can enter, she must answer the judges' question: What does she believe in? I am a writer, she tells them, I don't believe in anything. Her answers fail to satisfy the judges. Eventually, after many days, she has an answer. Frogs, she tells them. She believes in the frogs on the mudflats of the Dulgannon river, thousands and thousands of them, who burrow down deep underground to escape the heat of the sun until each has made a little tomb for itself, and there their hearts slow and their breathing stops and they die, in a manner of speaking. And they remain there, silent, until the rains come and rap on the little coffin lids and the hearts begin to beat again and the limbs start to twitch, and the dead awake. The mud softens and the frogs dig their way out and their voices – thousands and thousands of voices bellowing and croaking – rejoice to the high heavens. I believe in those little frogs, Elizabeth tells the judges, because they are real, because they exist, whether I believe in them or not.

I climb the stairs ahead of Peter. If someone were to turn and look up, they would see my husband marching me up to bed, and I, meekly, obeying. I might say this to Peter later. I might tell him that what I had wanted tonight – what he denied me – was the aftermath of Coetzee, his lingering aspect. I will tell him that the old illness is back, that night after night I am assailed by visions of animals, that I *see* the metal screws tightening on little heads, that I *hear* what every animal thinks when a man approaches: *What are you going to do to me? What are you going to do to my body, to my children?* I will say that I am losing empathy for my own species. I will tell him that I no longer regret the loss of our son, that I am glad I was spared motherhood, that my greatest fear was that I would gaze into my son's eyes and envisage the evil he might, one day, loose upon the world.

Step by step, I climb. I think of my notebook, inside my bag. I still have my thoughts. I still have my mind; no one can deny me my mind. I believe in frogs too, and the clay children of Pompeii and the infinite nights ahead. I remember the Aleph again, the tiny sphere that encloses the whole universe, that makes visible every point and every place and every act from every angle, and in every light.

My Little Pyromaniac

I had not thought of Kevin for a long time. Then, one evening last summer just after I'd moved in here, he came walking out of the house next door. I was getting out of my car, and there was just enough time for each of us to acknowledge the other, the way new neighbours do, before he got into his own car. I walked to my front door, holding myself carefully, aware of the woman and children coming behind him, then the thunk of car doors closing.

I stood in my hall, picturing the car moving along the street, the woman — his wife? — beside him, the boy and girl in the back; he, silent at the wheel, confounded by the sight of me after all these years, and the realisation that I was now living next door. And the slowly dawning thought that, from now on, we might, at any given moment, be only a few feet from each other, standing in our symmetrically positioned kitchens or bedrooms.

All the houses in this cul-de-sac are semi-detached, inhabited mostly by families with young children or teenagers. In the evenings the cars roll in, spilling out tired adults, children dragging coats and bags, sports gear, musical instruments. One evening, the little girl next door hopped out of Kevin's car dressed in a tutu. Her mother leaned into the back seat and took the child's bag and carried it into the house. She is a small, dark-haired woman, and appears to be much younger than Kevin. The boy is about ten, the girl perhaps seven. I have watched them closely – I am not entirely convinced these are Kevin's children.

When I was nineteen and still at university, I fell in love with Kevin. He was thirty-eight. He had a handsome, hewn face, a little like Warren Beatty's. He worked for a large investments company, and lived in a beautiful Victorian redbrick with lamplit rooms and stained-glass panels in the front door. He was often abroad on business, and sometimes a week or two would go by before I heard from him. Then we would meet and, if it suited him, I would stay over.

He would drop me off at college in his big car the next morning on his way to work or to the airport. Before I got out, I'd wait for him to say when we were to meet again. But he never did, and I carried a sickly feeling of loss and injury around with me all day. I'd let a few days pass, and then I'd dial his number at night and listen to the ringing at the other end, imagining the street light shining in his front door and the lovely ivory Bakelite on the hall table echoing through the house. Then, finally, a night would come when he would answer, and there would be a little pause after I said my name. He'd invite me over, but I would hesitate, say that I had lectures in the morning. I had to show some restraint. I was afraid he would catch something in my voice, or that even the Bakelite would betray me.

After we ended, I used to think I saw him coming towards me on the street, or entering, with other men in suits, expensive basement restaurants on St Stephen's Green at lunchtime on Fridays. Or, in more recent times, at the airport, when I'd come on those high shoeshine chairs on the way to the departure gates and have to do a double take, thinking it was Kevin sitting up there reading his newspaper while a young man polished his shoes. Once, about ten years ago, I was standing at a busy intersection near my apartment, trying to hail a taxi into town. It was a Thursday evening and darkness was falling, and all the passing taxis were occupied. I stood at the edge of the kerb to get the best view in all directions. Once or twice, I met the eyes of car drivers as they slowed to turn left. Then a large black jeep, a Range Rover, approached. There was something tentative about the way it slowed and something familiar about the shape of the driver that made my heart jump. I was sure it was him. I tried not to look, but as it drew level the passenger window slid down, and the man's eyes met mine. It was not Kevin. The man looked directly into my eyes, strangely, intently, and then suddenly I knew what he wanted. I shrank back and turned and hurried along the footpath to a bus stop, with nothing left in my legs but terror. At the bus shelter, I checked myself: my jeans and leather jacket, my shirt, my boots. What was it about me? Were my jeans too tight, was my hair too bright?

Was I standing too close to the kerb? Is there a line, a demarcation point, beyond which a woman standing on a kerb will be mistaken for a hooker?

I keep well back from kerbs now. My attachment to such shame still troubles me. It could have been him. There was something about Kevin – an arrogance, an authority, a furtiveness too. He was a man used to getting his own way, a man who might send out secret signs and demands to women, and expect them to acquiesce.

On a Sunday in November, a few months in, the relationship ended. I had cycled over to his house, bearing steaks and wine in my rucksack. He was out hiking on the Wicklow Mountains, and had left a key under a stone for me. I mooched around the rooms, opened drawers, touched his folded jumpers. I stood at his kitchen window and looked out at the old tree and the wrought-iron seat in the garden. I thought of him coming off the mountains, steadying himself against the car as he pulled off his boots, the damp and exhaustion of the day lodged in his bones, then the drive back to the city. I had a vision of the evening ahead, the steak and the wine, our conversation, and something in me exalted.

I tried to light a fire in the sitting room, but it wouldn't take. I found a drum of petrol in the shed, that he kept for his lawnmower. In my youth I had seen my brother and his friends light bonfires with petrol, so I built a pyre of coal and rolled-up newspapers in the grate. I held the drum carefully and poured the petrol over the coal and newspapers. I lit a match and held it to the coal, but before the flame even made contact, tongues of fire blazed up and leapt out at me, whipping at my legs, igniting the droplets of fuel on the hearth, on the rug, on the armrest of the sofa. I ran from the room, from the fireballs that erupted behind me, beating out a little flame on the leg of my jeans as I went.

The sound of crackling kindle still unnerves me, the mortification still scorches. For a long time I dreamt of little fires breaking out all over the place – in my shopping basket as I roamed supermarket aisles, in the nest of my piled-up hair, on my ring finger. I read somewhere that arsonists get an erotic charge and even sexual gratification from lighting fires. I can understand that – that moment of near annihilation, the juncture of sex and death, Eros and Thanatos. They like to watch fire for its beauty too, its aesthetic value. Once, I woke up on Kevin's sofa to find him watching me. He touched my cheek lightly, delicately. I was greatly moved. There must have been other moments of kindness and tenderness. Such moments would be worth having now, worth remembering.

I ran out of his house that day and rapped on the neighbour's door. The man – his name was Seán – came and put out the little fires with wet towels. Then he stood and inspected the room, and finally looked at me. A huge fire engine turned the corner onto the street at that moment and sent blue light strobes around the room.

In a frenzy of fear and adrenaline, I opened the windows, washed down the walls and surfaces, draped my cardigan over the armrest of the sofa. When Kevin came in, he never noticed a thing. He kissed me in the kitchen and went upstairs to shower. Later, I handed him a glass of wine and served up the steaks, and afterwards we carried our glasses to the front room. He sniffed the air, and threw coal on the fire, and it was this – the way he aimed the scuttle at the flames – that got to me, and I broke down and blurted out the whole story.

He will kneel now, I thought, and hold me and examine my hands and ensure that I am unharmed. But he did not move. My gaze fell to his feet and I remembered the flames licking at my heels and the hand of death on my back. I thought of the city and the dark night around us and I was filled with shame, and I couldn't wait to flee that house. He came and sat beside me and stroked my hair and whispered, 'My little pyromaniac,' and then he kissed me.

In those first days after seeing him last summer, I kept an approximate log of his comings and goings. The thought of meeting him again petrified me. I rehearsed a few banal words to say – about what a small world it really is, and how little he had changed in twenty years. But weeks went by, and then months, and we did not meet. It is astonishing how people can live in such close quarters and yet remain remote from one another. We passed in the street, sequestered behind the windscreens of our cars. We wheeled our bins, parallel to each other, out our driveways on Sunday nights. Then, gradually, as the months passed, something shifted. The heightened state of anxiety and anticipation in which I had held myself slowly dissipated. Aided by him, I think. By some understanding in him – and consideration for those around him, perhaps even for me — an understanding with which I would not previously have credited him.

He smokes now — I've seen the glow of his cigarette in the garden at night. Years ago, he kept an inhaler on his bathroom shelf, for occasional use only, he told me. He did not seem, at the time, the kind of person who might suffer from asthma. I have known asthma sufferers — they are delicate, uncertain, sometimes stunted. One evening last autumn, I watched him carry in the shopping bags and felt an appalling rush of affection for him. For his slow deliberate movements, and his ordinariness. Devoid of the big house and car and the trappings of his previous lifestyle, some power has been divested of him. Whatever the cause of his comedown in the world — whatever bad luck or financial loss he suffered — he has transmuted his circumstances, and is changed. In some obscure inner part of himself, he has changed.

I work from home now. I am a freelance copy editor, and I spend my days in an upstairs room at the back of my house poring over manuscripts sent by publishers. I love the close engagement with a text. I love the fine anatomy of a perfectly constructed sentence. I read each manuscript slowly, and insert, on almost every page, semi-colons, commas, dashes, linebreaks. So many punctuation marks shunned or misplaced, nowadays, that I hold myself in readiness — tense, rigid, nervous — anticipating the transgressions. Commas, for some reason, fare the worst. Their neglect almost grieves me. The spaces where they rightfully belong beckon to me, and I feel each space's ache for the tiny symbol, the cypher that gives form to a pause, a faint intake of breath, a remembrance.

From my desk, I have a view onto my garden and the gardens on either side, and, of course, the sky. The weather has been subject to sudden change this summer – cloud formations in chrome and magnesium shadow the ground some days. Then, wheeling skies and downpours, even lightning. There is something elemental about living in a property of my own, moored to one particular spot on earth, that I had not experienced before, that I had not reckoned on before moving in here.

Kevin keeps a dog, a German Shepherd, that constantly paces the perimeter of the garden. She drags her limbs round and round on the worn grass, then throws herself down in a corner. I know her habits now, the pattern of her rising and pacing and resting. She stands out in the rain and the lightning – there is no kennel. Occasionally, I take a kitchen stool into my garden and stand on it and lean over the wall. The dog rises on her hind legs and wags her tail, and whines. There, there, I say. I stroke her paws, her overgrown toenails. I feed her slices of bread and butter. I bring her water. She pricks up her ears at every sound – Kevin's car turning into the cul-de-sac in the evenings, the doors slamming, voices in the house. She wags her tail when the little girl comes out, and the little girl wags her index finger, orders the dog to sit, stand, lie. She drags her around by the collar, presses down on the small of the dog's back, tries to straddle her. Bold-dog, bold-dog, she says, in a staccato voice, if the dog moves, then slaps the dog in the face. *Bold-dog.* Slap-slap.

In the afternoons, I drive to Sandymount and walk along the strand until I reach the rocks. I come only when the tide is far out. Proximity to a high tide or a swelling ocean induces a kind of vertigo in me, an uneasy feeling that I will be pulled in, swallowed up, brought far from any shore. But I love the cry of seagulls, and the salt air. As I walk, I ponder the text I'm working on, turning over in my mind a particular clause or sentence that gives me pause. I meet elderly couples, dog walkers of all ages. Day after day, I see the same faces. I feel immense tenderness for old people, for their pale melancholy eyes, their thin wrinkled skin, their diminished stature. I see them again on nearby streets as I drive away, re-entering houses, returning to routines that keep time and death and the disquiet of twilight at bay. There is an old man with whom I sometimes exchange a few words. He is tall, white-haired, patrician – I do not know his name, or anything about him. One of his dogs is called Laika. She is named after the dog sent into space on Sputnik 2 – a stray from the Moscow streets, chosen for the project because of her placid nature, he told me. I found her photograph on the internet – she is strapped into a leather harness just before take-off, her eyes eager and shining, her ears pricked up.

The moon is huge these nights, a supermoon, the weatherman says, an optical illusion. If I mute my TV, I can hear Kevin's through the living-room walls. Ad jingles, the signature tune of the *Nine O'Clock* news. Last night I watched the pounding of Gaza by F16s, trolleys racing along hospital corridors, ribbons of shrapnel on the faces of children. After midnight, I climbed the stairs and looked out my bedroom window at the moon. Pulling all of Earth's tides, Earth's energy, I thought, causing an exodus of vitality. I thought of Kevin on the other side of the wall, his head next to his wife's, his children asleep nearby. If this *is* his wife, if these are his children. I lay down and thought about the simultaneous existence of our private lives, and how we slip into our private sleep, visited by dreams and fragments from the past, and how the same darkness, the same night, envelops us both, and yet there is no name for what any of this is. There is nothing to explain how we — humans — can, one minute, lie down and reveal our most secret vulnerable selves to each other, greet the other's soul in the sex act, and then, the next minute, or the next day or week or month, part, and go separately into the world as if we are strangers, as if we have not left a burn on the other.

I awoke at some point in the night, disturbed by something — an apprehension. My window was open a little, and I heard a voice, low and tight and angry. *Shut up. Shut up.* I saw him, below, in the moonlight. He brought his cigarette to his mouth. The dog whined, her head held low, timid. The cigarette smoke curled from his mouth, and the dog whined again. *Shut up. Shut the fuck up, I said.* He swung his open palm and struck the side of her head with great force. Before she knew what had happened, before her head had righted itself, he struck again, and she yelped and slunk away into the shadows.

Long after he had gone inside, she emerged out into the moonlight and stood very still, staring at the ground. I pictured the tender insides of her head in slight disarray. Her vision blurred, the world warped, all sounds surreal. She might need to tilt her head to restore the balance of fluid in her inner ear, or resettle tiny cerebral folds into skull cavities, eyes into sockets. There might be a little bleed, a swelling, a cerebral oedema. The brain might soften, and if it does, I thought, then surely that will be a blessing, bringing, as it will, forgetfulness. She began to pace the worn grass. I watched her for a long time. I am aware of her always, there, at the edge of my being. Suppose there had been no petrol in his shed that day. Suppose I had not set fire to his house, or run away in shame. That might have been my house. Those might have been my children. This might have been my dog.

There were no sudden showers or elemental lightning today. Not a leaf stirred and only the postman and a cat prowling on the footpath disturbed the stillness of the street. I took the stool into the garden and hoicked myself up on the wall, and jumped down into Kevin's garden. The dog came, and I fell to my knees and threw my arms around her neck. Little by little, she let her body recline against mine, and sighed deeply. A few minutes passed. I know now that in our hour of need, set with a seemingly impossible task, we become, like the Greek heroes, suddenly imbued with extraordinary strength. I stood and scooped her up in my arms, lifted her high. I bore her weight with ease and grace and, as I raised her up, I felt myself raised too, she and I airborne as one, until her paws grasped the top of the wall and her weight left me, and she was gone, over the top, down into my garden.

I moved with serene calm and certainty, as if it were all preordained. I crossed Kevin's patio to the side gate, slid back the bolt, let it swing open. I crossed again and climbed – one, two, three – up onto the oil tank set against the wall, and jumped down into my own garden. The dog followed me inside, and sat at my feet, and I laid a bowl of cereal and milk on the floor for her. I picked up my keys, and went out and reversed my car up close to the front door, and opened the boot. I took the belt from my jeans and slid it under the dog's collar and led her through the hall, and willingly she came.

Shh, it's okay, I said, as I drove. She was silent, closed up in the dark behind me, but I talked anyway. All the way to Sandymount, I talked. Nearly there now, I said, as we approached the street and the wooden door set into the wall that I had seen the old man enter. And still I talked. Good girl. I rang the bell and there came, instantly, the sound of dogs barking. When he opened the door, he frowned and looked at her, then at me. Behind him, a gravel courtyard, an ivy-covered house.

'You might not remember me,' I said. 'We met on the strand a few times.'

He nodded slowly, said nothing.

'This one needs a home,' I said. I told him, briefly, of her life. Still he said nothing, just stepped back, let the door fall open, let me relinquish her into his yard.

It was Laika, the Moscow stray, I conjured on the way home. Alone in the cabin, moving through the cold and the dark, amid shoals of cosmic dust, clusters of beryllium suns. The night before the launch, one of the scientists took her home to play with his children. He wanted to do something nice for her. I did this for Kevin, I tell myself, as I turn onto the canal. I did it to save his children from the moment when she might turn on them. But I didn't. I did it for her. I did it for me.

His car is pulling into the driveway now. I wait. Five, six, seven . . . ten minutes pass on the display of my DVD player. The children are first onto the street. Then Kevin and the woman emerge. He says something to her and signals to the houses opposite and then crosses, diagonally, to the other side. The girl runs after him, and he takes her hand and I see, instantly, the resemblance, the synchronicity, the physical resonance. They begin at the house in the corner. He raises a hand to knock.

My doorbell rings. It is the woman, with the boy beside her.

'Have you seen our dog?' she asks. Her voice is stern, urgent.

I shake my head, frown, wait for her to elaborate. 'No,' I say.

'She's gone. The side gate was open when we got home and she was gone.' Her eyes are drilling mine.

'She's probably not far away,' I say. 'She probably just wandered off.'

The woman shakes her head. 'The gate was bolted – someone must have opened it . . . She wouldn't know her way home.'

I keep my eyes on her. My heart is pounding. You are not worthy of a dog, I think. You people.

The boy is staring at me. He gives me a chill, and I turn back to his mother.

'Did you see anything unusual today?' she asks. 'Anyone calling to our house, or anything?'

I am aware of Kevin on the driveway of the house opposite. Again I shake my head. 'No,' I say. 'I was out for a few hours in the morning. But I was in all afternoon. I didn't see anything.' Across the street nobody answers and Kevin turns and begins to walk out the driveway.

She starts to move away. 'If you remember anything, will you let us know, please? The children are very upset. Someone must have seen something – someone must have let her out, or taken her.'

The boy does not immediately turn. His lingering disconcerts me, and I look away, and then back again at his pale anxious face. We regard each other for a moment, and I think he is going to speak. There is something he wants to say, something he wants me to decipher – it is there, a straining in his eyes: distress or sorrow or pleading. He lets out a sigh, then turns and follows his mother, and before I have my door fully closed he is calling across the street. *Kevin.* I step into my living room and watch them stand and confer in the middle of the street. Kevin raises his hand and rubs his forehead. He is looking in this direction, straight in the window at me, and our eyes meet. All that is within him, all he has ever seen and felt and known, all of time past, time fallen, is funnelled into this moment. Nothing is erased. The eye remembers everything.

I sit in the twilight with the TV on mute. Bombs are raining down on Gaza again. She will return tomorrow, that woman. And the boy. I try to imagine what it was it he wanted of me? To give him back the dog? To relieve him of his sorrow? To be rescued?

I switch off the TV and sit in the dark. I think of the dog in Sandymount, pacing the yard, then standing, staring at the ground as the moon rises above her.

The Choc-Ice Woman

Frances had never been in a hearse before. Mr O'Shea, the undertaker, pulled out into traffic and set off down North Circular Road, past the women's wing of Mountjoy Prison, and the library at Eglinton Terrace where she had been a librarian for twelve years before her retirement. The road forked at St Peter's Church, and they picked up speed approaching the gates at Phoenix Park. She was grateful for the hum of the engine, the city outside. She kept herself apart, mentally, from Mr O'Shea. She forgot, briefly, about the coffin with the remains of her brother Denis behind her head until the hearse braked going downhill on Infirmary Road and she had a vision of it crashing through the glass partition and slamming into them.

'Are you all right there?' Mr O'Shea asked at the traffic lights.

'I am, thanks,' she replied.

'Is it warm enough – would you like me to turn up the heat?'

'I'm fine, thanks,' she said. He put the hearse in gear and turned right. 'I'm sorry about this,' she added. 'I'm sure you'd much prefer to be on your own for the journey.'

There had been a moment of confusion outside the hospital morgue when she announced her intention to travel in the hearse. The coffin had already been loaded, and Mr O'Shea had completed the paperwork, when she and her husband Frank arrived. He shook hands and sympathised with them.

'I'm very sorry for your loss,' he said. 'I put the notice and the funeral arrangements on RIP.ie this morning before I left.'

Frances nodded her thanks, and they stood awkwardly for a few moments.

'We can head off so, if ye're ready?' Mr O'Shea said.

'I'll go in the hearse with you,' she said suddenly. It had come out of nowhere.

Mr O'Shea looked at her and then at Frank, a little alarmed. Without another word, she went around to the passenger side of the hearse and got in.

They were crossing the Liffey at Islandbridge now.

'I know it's usually a man from the family that travels in the hearse,' she continued, 'or at least that used to be the tradition. But I don't drive, you see, so if Frank went with you, there'd be no one to drive the car home.'

'That's no problem at all,' Mr O'Shea said. 'And as for traditions, aren't they changing all the time?'

He checked the rear-view mirror, then the wing mirror. 'Frank is close enough behind us anyway. We'll probably get separated along the way but what harm, aren't we all going to the same place?'

She had enough of the talking now. If she had gone with Frank, there would have been little talk on the journey.

'We'll be on the motorway shortly,' Mr O'Shea said. They were passing Inchicore. An old woman, pulling a wheelie shopper, stopped at a letterbox. 'We should be in Kerry by five o'clock, all going well.'

The woman was trying to push a brown package into the letterbox, her white hair tossing wildly in the wind.

'Is that all right?' Mr O'Shea asked.

'Yes, yes.'

'And if you feel like a break any time along the way,' he said, 'just say the word and we can stop.'

The more he talked, the harder it would be to keep herself separate.

'The woman who does the embalming,' he said, a little tentatively, 'will be coming in at half past six. How would ye be fixed . . . would ye be able to get his clothes in to us then?'

Denis's suit hung in his wardrobe for decades. He had last worn it to the funerals of their parents. He had not attended their brother Patrick's funeral.

'Any time before seven is fine,' Mr O'Shea added. 'If I'm not there myself, Anne my wife will take them in.'

'That's no problem. Frank will drop them in.'

A strange occupation for a woman, embalming, she thought. Surely two people are needed to lift and move a body. She wondered if Mr O'Shea's wife assisted. The two women packing cotton wool into orifices.

71

'Are all corpses embalmed?' she asked. 'Is it absolutely necessary?'

'Well, I suppose it's not *absolutely* necessary. Some cultures don't do it, but then they tend to bury their dead very quickly. It's the done thing, nowadays. In the western world anyway. It makes things a lot easier for the family, it removes a lot of the difficulties and the . . . unpleasantness. It's best for the deceased too.'

Stitching up the tongue? I don't think so, Frances wanted to say.

She had googled the process when Patrick died, and had been shocked by what she read. If limbs need to be straightened, the tendons or ligaments are cut. Internal organs are punctured to prevent them from swelling up with gas. The heart is drained of liquid. The embalming itself involves a machine pumping pink fluid into the body for forty-five minutes. Frances could not recall if the blood is removed beforehand, and if not, how does the body accommodate all that liquid? Little plastic caps are fitted underneath the eyelids to keep the natural shape before the eyelids are glued shut. Even the mouth is sewn shut. They put a suture in the jaw – inside the mouth – or they draw a threaded needle through the bottom lip, then up under the top lip, through the septum and down into the mouth again. One website said tacks are anchored in the jawbone, and these tacks have wires which are then twisted to keep the mouth shut.

'Will I send in his socks and – everything?' she asked.

'Yes, everything, except the shoes. We don't usually put shoes on.'

The light would be fading when they got to Castleisland. She and Frank would enter Mr O'Shea's premises and follow him through a warren of little rooms and corridors to a storeroom out the back. There, from a selection of four or five, they would choose a coffin for Denis, as they had for Patrick four years ago, before driving the three miles out home. Later Frank would drive back to town with Denis's clothes, and she would be alone for a while, and able to breathe again. The following evening, Denis would lie in repose in O'Shea's Funeral Home between six and eight o'clock, before being removed to the church ahead of the funeral Mass the next morning. Friends, neighbours and distant relatives would file past the open coffin all evening, sympathising with Frances and then Frank, squeezing Frances's hand until her fingers hurt.

For two weeks she had been at Denis's bedside in the Mater Hospital, leaving only after ten p.m. to return to her B&B on Drumcondra Road. In the last two days he had not spoken or opened his eyes, and his breathing grew shallower and shallower. She had had an inkling last night, and felt she should stay longer, but the nurse assured her that he could last for several more days. Before she got to the B&B, her phone rang. She hurried back, but it was over, and he had been moved to a private room with tealights and a crucifix placed on the side table, and a leaflet for bereaved relatives. They had stretched a flesh-coloured band, like an elastic stocking, around his head to keep his mouth closed. She kissed the top of his head and touched his hands and his nose, expecting to feel something. She thought of him as no longer alive, but not yet dead. She whispered his name, but it sounded contrived. Denis and Patrick were twins, twelve years older than Frances. Her mother had suffered several miscarriages between their birth and hers. In her childhood, Denis was a fleeting presence. Home from Dublin one Christmas when she was eight or nine, he brought her a red plastic tea set, six Jaffa oranges wrapped individually in tissue paper, and a box of cornflakes, because cornflakes were a rare treat then. Not long afterwards, he came home for good, and seldom left his room.

Already, he was changing before her eyes. His face was collapsing inwards, and his nose seemed more pointed, like a bird's beak. The body was dissolving, every cell was disintegrating. Gravity was drawing his blood to his back, where it would pool and congeal. Soon rigor mortis would set in. His soul had probably left his body by now, she thought. Where was she – running down Drumcondra Road or along Dorset Street – when that happened? So many mysteries. Did his blood ebb to a halt at the same time as consciousness shut down? It is easier to track the body's exit than the exit of the mind. And there is no knowing what the mind suffers in the final hours and minutes. Just before her mother took her last breath, she opened her eyes wide with a petrified look, as if seeing something terrible, but twenty-four hours later her face was serene, as if all the pain of existence had left her.

A nurse arrived to say they would soon need to take Denis to the morgue. Frances went down to the foyer and called Frank. 'Denis is gone,' she said. She did not wait for his response. 'Will you ring O'Shea to come up and bring him home tomorrow?'

Frank was silent for a few moments. 'I'm sorry, Frances.'

'And ring the priest as well.'

'Will I come up tonight?' he asked.

'No, wait till the morning.'

Every morning for twelve years she had walked down Drumcondra Road on her way to work in the library in Phibsborough. The walk took forty-five minutes, and brought her past St Patrick's College where Denis had trained as a teacher more than fifty years before, then up the hill past the Archbishop's Palace and along Dorset Street before she turned right onto North Circular Road at the Ulster Bank. She arrived at the library an hour before opening time and put out the newspapers and latest magazines, logged returns and worked at her computer, checking orders and book club requests. She had worked alongside first one, then another assistant librarian, but never developed close friendships with either. At lunchtime during the summer months she sat on the grass in the little park behind the library and read her book and ate her sandwich. Behind her, the wall of the young offenders' prison rose thirty feet high. Often, a siren wailed in the distance and her mind drifted to the unfortunate boys on the other side of the wall. The library was busiest in the afternoons when the schoolchildren arrived. She did not mind the older students, but she barely tolerated children in her library. She insisted on silence, and did little to encourage them, other than coordinating a monthly Storytime slot facilitated by a local children's author. She abhorred the way libraries had changed. The bigger city libraries resembled community centres or crèches, such was the level of noise and activity – not just caused by shrieking babies and ringing phones, but the facilitation of everything from art classes to mother-and-toddler mornings. Since when can toddlers read, Frances wanted to know? After work, she locked up and walked up to Dorset Street, took the 16A bus to the Collins Avenue junction, and walked the last four hundred metres to her front door.

One day four years ago, on the eve of Frances's sixtieth birthday, Patrick came in from the fields in Kerry, stood in the middle of the kitchen and collapsed. Denis went to the hall, picked up the phone and called Frances in the library. 'I think Patrick is gone,' he said.

For a while after Patrick's death, Frances and Frank travelled down from Dublin every weekend. But Denis could not be left alone and so, at the age of sixty and after thirty-nine years' service with Dublin City Libraries, Frances retired from her job and moved back home to Kerry. Within months Frank too retired, and they sold the house in Whitehall, and the move became permanent. Still reeling from the loss of Patrick, she leased out the farm to a local man, and tried to restore the routine Denis had always known. She knew the shape of his days, his preference for plain food, his need for solitude, and these she could provide. But she could not replace Patrick, and though Denis never mentioned him or showed any outward sign of grief, Frances was certain he was pining for his twin brother's presence in the house. Frank drove Denis to the library in town every fortnight and did his best to help. Frances never asked what, if anything, they talked about on these journeys. Denis rarely spoke anyway, and in the thirty years they had known each other, she doubted if Frank and Denis had ever had a conversation, neither man knowing how to talk to the other.

They were on the motorway through Kildare, then Laois. Farmhouses appeared on hills, sheds and outhouses nestled in behind them, the fields bare now in the dead of winter. Denis was behind her, his head inches from her own, his worn little body resting on the satin lining of the coffin. Or maybe there was no satin. Maybe this was a workhorse coffin, for transport purposes only. Denis might be in a body bag, still in his stained pyjamas, zipped up from his bony white feet to the top of his head. The odours of a decomposing body would, she thought, still leak out, despite the body bag, and leave a scent in the coffin for the next incumbent. She read somewhere that the reason dogs go crazy when they're muzzled at the vet's is because the scents of other dogs suddenly thrust on their faces is overwhelming, sending them into a frenzy of fear and panic.

Mr O'Shea's mobile phone, propped on the dashboard, vibrated, startling her. He tapped it quickly. 'Sorry about that,' he said.

A few moments later it vibrated again, and again he apologised. 'That's my daughter. Young people! It's always urgent with them, isn't it?' He switched the phone off.

'How old is your daughter?' Frances asked.

'Sally. She's nineteen. She's actually on her way home now for the weekend. She's in college in Dublin.'

'What is she studying?'

'Medicine. She's in second year in UCD.'

'You must be very proud of her.'

It struck her that Mr O'Shea might have planned to take his daughter home in the hearse, that it might be a regular arrangement whenever he was tasked with bringing the dead of Castleisland home from Dublin. With a contingency in place: *If you can't reach me, it means I have a family member with me, so take the train.*

Mr O'Shea adjusted the rear-view mirror, then checked his wing mirror. 'I think we've lost Frank,' he said.

Not far out of the city, before hitting the motorway, Frank would have pulled over at a service station, filled up with fuel, bought a newspaper, tea, a breakfast roll and a bar of chocolate. On a day like this, he couldn't very well linger on the forecourt. Service stations – along with shopping centres and suburban housing estates – were, Frances used to imagine, one of his pick-up spots for women. She'd picture him parking off to the side, near the service area, with his tea and breakfast roll, the racing page open on the steering wheel, keeping an eye out for a lone woman emerging from the shop, then tracking her until she – game, like him, for a motorway fling – met his eye. There might be nothing said, just a look. The woman would pull over to check her tyres and Frank would, naturally, offer his help. Or in some instances he might simply tail the woman out of the service station, drive steadily in the lane alongside her until she turned her head, and a look was exchanged. They were all the same, these women, it didn't matter where he found them; they were all like Frank.

Frank had started out as her lodger over thirty years ago. Soon after she bought the house off Collins Avenue, she advertised the two spare bedrooms to rent, to help with the mortgage repayments. When he walked through the door – tall, broad, handsome, with dark curly hair – and when she heard his country accent and saw his shy, polite manner, her heart flipped. And then there was the coincidence of his name. He worked with the gas board installing, servicing and repairing gas boilers. A young teacher from Clare took the other room. Frances split the bills three ways, set the house rules and stuck a cleaning rota on the fridge. Frank had a light footprint. He parked his van out on the road and was gone every morning before eight. He was clean and tidy and quiet; he hoovered his room every Saturday, was discreet with his laundry, paid his rent on time and was never drunk. He avoided conversation and eye contact, and in those rare times when he did speak, Frances detected an endearing uncertainty in him. After a year, the young teacher moved out and Frances and Frank fell to cooking together in the evenings. She began to look forward to their meals, and their time alone. She told him about Kerry, her twin brothers, her widowed mother. For months Frank offered nothing, and she thought him inscrutable. But, little by little, over the winter evenings, she learned the outline of his life. He had been placed in an orphanage very early on and, at the age of six, was fostered out to a farmer and his wife in Co. Kilkenny. At fifteen he started an apprenticeship with a local plumber, and he came to Dublin at seventeen. He knew nothing about his birth mother, other than the name on his birth cert, and when Frances gently enquired if he was not curious about her or his father, he shook his head. She had the impression of a man who did not want to delve into the past, a man who easily forgave and forgot the failings of others. He voiced no strong opinions, held no political allegiance and was visibly uncomfortable with gossip. Whenever he spoke of workmates or clients or his employer, it was always with equanimity. One Saturday evening after they had washed up the dishes, he folded the tea towel and stood behind a chair and asked her if she'd like to go down to the Viscount for a drink.

She had not expected to love a man so completely different to her father and her brothers, a man without family – she for whom family was foremost in her life; a man without any obvious origins, as if he had simply materialised on earth when he crossed her threshold. She used to imagine scenes from his childhood – she had watched such scenes in films and documentaries: eager, hopeful children in orphanages lined up for inspection by visitors, then watching as the pretty ones are chosen and driven away to begin their new lives. She was so haunted by one scene – an American woman asking a little boy to roll up his sleeves, then moving on to the next child when she sees his ringworm – that she had to remind herself that Frank was not that boy. Whenever she tried to nudge Frank into investigating his origins, he shook his head. He told her that, as a young man going to dances, whenever he told a girl about his background, the girl would have nothing more to do with him. There were moments when this absence of a past or a solid identity had bothered Frances, but then she would remember the little boy he once was, and she would be ambushed by a surge of love that flowed from her spine, down through her arms and hands, and weakened her.

She was thirty-four and Frank was thirty-two when they married. She knew she was no beauty – tall, thin and angular, with little in the way of hips or bosom – but neither this nor the plainness of her dress – she favoured dark trousers, cream or white blouses, navy or wine cardigans – had seemed to matter to Frank. Frances's value lay not in her looks, but in her love for Frank, and in her good job, her intelligence, her home ownership. Besides, she was convinced that Frank's lineage must be notable; how else but genetics to explain his looks, his good manners, his work ethic, and had he not made something of himself despite his beginnings? Whenever little doubts or signs of deprivation in him troubled her, she would quell them by recalling an incident from their honeymoon. They were on a street in Edinburgh and Frank went to buy a lottery ticket. 'Get me a Bounty bar, if they have them,' she said. When he came out of the shop and handed her the Bounty, he said, 'I don't know how you eat those things. I *hate* coconut.' Such a strong word from Frank. They sat in a park, and he told her that Kelly, the farmer who had fostered him as a boy, always had sweets, which he never shared with Frank. One day Frank saw a sweet – an Emerald – on the floor of the tractor. He didn't dare pick it up in front of the farmer. He crept out that night and retrieved the sweet and hid behind the cowshed and sucked it very slowly, to make it last.

That first year was the heyday of their marriage. She added his name to the deeds of the house. Together they painted the house, built raised beds in the back garden. On summer evenings they took walks on Dollymount Strand or drove out to Howth and ate fish and chips on the pier. That September they took a holiday in Greece because Frances had always wanted to visit the oracle at Delphi. She hoped that Frank might take up reading and brought along a thriller from the library, but when she saw his eyelids droop and his head drop, she smiled and took the book away. Frank rarely expressed needs or wants or wishes of his own, a trait, Frances assumed, that had developed early in his life when he learned to expect nothing from anyone. They bought a car and went to Kerry regularly. Her mother liked Frank and jokingly conspired against Frances, complaining about her dress sense or her regimental lifestyle. 'Why are you covering yourself up?' her mother would ask. 'And you so slim, you can wear anything. But no, never a bit of colour on you!' Then she'd turn to Frank. 'I have only the one daughter, Frank, and she dresses like a nun. Maybe you can get her to change.'

In those early years, Frances and Frank spent most of their holidays in Kerry. On these trips, Frances cleaned the house from top to bottom – stripped beds, cleared cupboards, polished furniture, washed curtains and walls and windows, while outside Frank painted gates, cleaned gutters, trimmed hedges, mowed the grass. Frances trusted Frank with these chores; he was a capable and neat workman, and she was her most relaxed and cheerful self during these weeks of industrious endeavours.

She expected they would have children quickly and easily. After two years, tests revealed blocked fallopian tubes, and though she had never remembered having had symptoms, the condition was attributed to suspected peritonitis following an appendix operation when she was twenty-one. She underwent surgery to unblock the tubes and a year later suffered an ectopic pregnancy, followed in subsequent years by two miscarriages, the latter of which occurred in the sixth month. That is a long time ago now, and though Frank showed little emotion at the time, she believed then that his outer display of stoicism was his way of supporting her, and that, inside, he was as bereft as she was.

Now she is no longer sure that Frank experiences grief – or any emotion for that matter – in the manner that she and, she assumes, others experience it. Still, even now and after everything that has happened, she must admit that, with the exception of Denis, she has never known anyone as peaceable as Frank. In all their years together, he never raised his voice or spoke harshly to her, or displayed the least flicker of irritation. She had always considered herself a kind person, if a little sharp at times, but there were moments when Frank's passivity tested the limits of her patience. During an argument, or what should have naturally developed into an argument, he avoided looking at her and said almost nothing, so that she failed to find purchase. She'd goad him, accuse him of stubbornness, of stonewalling her, until he'd shake his head and put his hand out and plead with her not to be cross, that this — whatever the issue was — didn't matter. 'This isn't normal,' she'd cry. 'Why don't you ever get angry? Where do you put your anger?'

One evening, three or four years into the marriage, Frank told her of an incident at work when his boss had been rude and dismissive to him.

'Why didn't you stand up for yourself?' she demanded, furious. 'Why do you always let people walk all over you? Jesus Christ, what's wrong with you? Say something, don't just sit there like some . . . dumb animal.'

He was sitting at the kitchen table. 'I'm sorry if I'm not the man you want me to be,' he said.

He had never spoken like this. She waited, her heart pounding.

'You know how I told you I was fostered to the Kellys when I was six? Well, I saw what anger did in that house. Tom Kelly was a brute. And worse when he got into a rage.' He shook his head. 'There's nothing to be gained from anger, Frances.'

'What happened? Was he a brute to you?'

'He was a brute to everyone and everything. Me, the wife, the dog. I ate and slept in the back kitchen — I had a little bed that I folded away every morning. I wasn't allowed into the kitchen, except to put turf in the range. I got the leftover scraps – myself and the dog got the same food. He wouldn't let her give me proper meals. She'd give me nice things when he was gone to the mart or somewhere. Homemade bread and jam, a bit of meat. He wouldn't allow the dog inside, but I used to sneak him in at night and he'd lie beside me. Charlie. The loveliest dog you ever saw. And the brute shot him.'

'Jesus, Frank. Why did he shoot him?'

'Because Charlie knocked over a bucket of milk, that's why. That's what anger does.'

Mr O'Shea cleared his throat. His pale hands were resting on the steering wheel. Why had it surprised her that he was married, and had children? Because of his occupation, because it is hard to imagine a man who touches the dead every day being red-blooded and carnal? She doubted he had a strong libido. She can tell men like that now; they give off the whiff. She loathes people with big appetites – over-eaters and drinkers, loud, gluttonous, noisy people with no self-control and no desire to refine themselves. Wanton, swollen bodies, pulsating with lust. Rutting like animals. That is the kind of husband she has. *Base* was the word that occurred to her years ago when his carry-on first came to light. Base appetites and instincts. He had kept that side of himself hidden from her, but that is who he is. God knows who he has slept with, whose genitals he has slithered out of.

'I don't think I ever met Denis,' Mr O'Shea said. 'Was he long sick?'

'No, just a few months. He didn't go out much. He was always very delicate. The cancer was well advanced when they found it.'

'He went fast, Lord have mercy on him.'

'He did. That's the way he'd have wanted it.'

'It's always hard to lose a loved one.'

She liked that he had used Denis's name. She thought they might travel the whole journey without using each other's name.

'Very sad, and he a young man,' he continued.

'He was seventy-six.'

Mr O'Shea shot her a look. 'Seventy-six?'

She nodded. 'Seventy-seven next month. He was Patrick's twin.'

Mr O'Shea frowned, then checked the wing mirrors.

'He used to be a teacher, years ago,' she said.

Mr O'Shea stared ahead, as if he had not heard her.

Teaching had not suited Denis. Frances was about ten when he came back from Dublin for good. She was given to understand that Denis's gentle nature was ill-suited to the rough and tumble of the classroom. He spent his days in his bedroom after that, resting and reading, her mother bringing him his meals and his tablets, his laundered clothes, a tonic to build him up. When Frances helped her mother change the bed linen, she read the titles on his book shelves. *The Complete Works of Shakespeare*, *Paradise Lost*,

The History of the Decline and Fall of the Roman Empire, The Collected Poems of John Donne. Whenever she met Denis on the landing, he smiled and touched her head lightly, like a priest might do. No demands were ever made of him — it was Patrick who worked the farm with their father. Once a fortnight, Patrick drove Denis to the library in Castleisland where he spent an hour or more selecting books from the shelves. When Miss Downey, the elderly librarian, retired in 1996, Denis did not visit the library for over a year. In 2008, when the old library closed and a brand new library opened on Station Road, he absented himself again, until Patrick coaxed him back.

During Frances's teenage years, Denis left novels at her bedroom door — *Moby-Dick, Pride and Prejudice, Silas Marner.* They rarely spoke, his remoteness causing her to be a little afraid of him in those years. At night when they were all in bed, she heard him going downstairs. She was an adult before she understood he had had some kind of breakdown. She wondered if some girl had broken his heart. Once, about ten years ago, she came upon him sitting on a tree stump looking out over the fields with his back to her. He was very still. A wood pigeon landed on the stone wall to his left, and he turned his head slightly to watch it, and in the neutral way he observed the pigeon in those moments, she had a sudden realisation of his nature: his absolute surrender and acceptance of things the way they are. It was the way he observed everything — devoid of need or memory or rapture. Every day he moved as if senseless, formless, bodiless. He might be flotsam one minute, or pigeon, or air.

In the days after his burial, Frances would enter his room and go through his belongings. She had never questioned her mother about his breakdown, and she did not expect to find anything that would shed light on the past. In recent years she had considered various possibilities – that he might have been gay, or that something terrible was visited upon him, or even, on days when all kinds of fears populated her mind, that *he* had visited something terrible on someone else – a child, for instance.

It is Denis she credits with giving her a love of books and a glimpse of the life of the mind. In her first posting to Pembroke Library, old Miss Symms, the senior librarian, took Frances under her wing and, in less than two years, taught her how to read with an open mind, how to discern good writing from bad and trust her own artistic sensibility. She delivered to Frances a literary education that rivalled that offered by most universities, so that by the time she left that post, Frances could make a good fist of describing symbolist poetry or explaining why James Joyce or Virginia Woolf or William Faulkner mattered. She came to read Kafka and Isaac Babel and Chekhov with her own naïve but wily eye, and though these writers wrote of distant landscapes and lives that were far removed from her own she found an affinity with the minds of the characters on the page.

She read the biographies too, and would come upon little titbits that delighted her, like the fact that Joyce had kept two parakeets in his Paris flat, or that Robert Musil had once been a librarian. Over the decades, she continued to watch and learn from the book lovers and aesthetes who frequently her libraries – middle-aged, bluestocking ladies, rakish young men and intense young women whose clothes and hair indicated they cared little for grooming and who, at times, had to be gently reminded that the library would close in five minutes – and took note of the books they read and the journals they requested. One winter, a Dutch student named Thomas Bakker began to appear in her library on Friday evenings. He was thin and pale, with fair to reddish hair and high cheekbones. She saw him, one evening after she'd locked up, hunched against the wind on the street in Phibsborough, looking like a man from another century. He requested books which she had to call in from other libraries – titles by Robert Walser and Joseph Roth. When he returned the books, she took them home, one by one, and read them. Robert Musil's stories made the greatest impression on her, stories of young urban men – students and engineers and geologists – who headed out of the city on work assignments in bleak valleys where they seduced peasant girls. The stories were pervaded with sickness and death and what the young men thought of as love. They weighed on Frances and threw a pall over her, but she kept being drawn back to them, perhaps because she had been a country girl herself. There was something about the Dutch student that made her feel protective, though she never once had a conversation with him, and he was gone by spring. But she always associated Musil's stories with him. In her mind, too, she somehow associates them with Frank, with the grim, miserable landscape of his childhood. And the sex – there was always sex in Musil's stories; the sexual act had an almost religious fervour, and the men experienced something like a mystical union with the girls, but had little regard or pity for the girls' feelings or futures. Those poor girls, Frances thought, hoping for love, thinking they were truly favoured by the men.

They were coming off the motorway. She turned to Mr O'Shea.

'We'll have to stop,' he said, a little agitated. 'I'm afraid I might have collected the wrong remains at the morgue.'

She looked at him, and waited.

'I don't know for certain,' he said, 'but when you said your brother was seventy-six, I got a shock. It's a much younger man I collected, I'm sure of that. The name on the paperwork was correct, Denis Linnane, but . . . I'm very sorry about this, but I'll have to open the coffin and check. There's no point in continuing on until I do. Do you want to call Frank? He can link up with us and can check with me. It'd be too upsetting for you.'

She shook her head. 'No, it's all right. I can do it.'

'It's not the easiest thing, so—'

'I'll do it.'

They were on the outskirts of a town.

'This is Roscrea we're coming into,' he said. 'I know the church here, there's trees all around it, so it'll be private. A service station is no place for a job like this.'

The church spire came into view and Mr O'Shea turned the hearse into a churchyard surrounded by cypress and yew trees. He drove around the back of the church, and stopped.

'It'll take me a few minutes to get set up. Maybe you'd wait in the church, or go for a walk up the town or something. Whatever is the easiest for yourself. I'm very sorry about this.'

He would need to roll out the coffin and make Denis presentable. If, indeed, it was Denis.

'I'll walk up the town.'

'If you can give me ten or fifteen minutes.'

She put on a woollen hat and scarf and walked along the street and into a square with a tree and a stone fountain. She sat on a bench. They might have ferried a stranger's corpse all this way, she thought. A young woman in a puffer coat came and sat on a nearby bench, then lit a cigarette and became engrossed in her phone. The smell of the cigarette gave Frances a sudden longing. She had smoked in her youth – never more than ten a day – and quit when she was thirty. She started smoking the occasional cigarette again after the discovery about Frank, and then quit again four years ago after moving to Kerry. She had hoped the move to Kerry would herald a new start for them, that it would remove Frank from temptation. But a way will always be found and after six months Frank was back on the road again, working part-time with the local heating contractor. Age had not, as she had hoped, dimmed desire in Frank and soon she began to recognise the old patterns of deceit. She read an interview once with a woman in her late sixties who had had a total hysterectomy, and was grateful for the side effects. All her life she had had a monstrous libido, which had wreaked havoc on herself and her family in the form of affairs. Now, finally, after a lifetime of uncontrollable desire, the woman had peace.

It was on the 16A bus one summer's evening as it crawled through Drumcondra, that she discovered Frank's betrayal. A Thursday evening, just before the June bank holiday weekend. From her seat, she looked across the road at Thunder's Bakery, reminding herself that she had ordered a cake for collection the following evening to take to Kerry. As she shifted her gaze, her eyes registered a Bord Gáis van a little ahead in the lane alongside the bus. It was the little yellow sticker on the back door – a smiley character giving the thumbs-up sign – that caught her attention. That's Frank, she thought, happily, and leaned forward, ready to wave as the bus drew level. And in the space of about five seconds and in a distance of about five yards, her whole self began to slide sideways. A bare forearm rested on the passenger window. In the passenger seat sat a woman, her profile and short dark hair visible to Frances from her higher perch. The woman was talking, then laughing. She raised a choc-ice to her mouth and licked it. Then she stretched out her arm and Frank's face came into view and then Frank's tongue appeared, licking the woman's choc-ice.

Later, when he came in, she never pretended a thing. He went upstairs and showered as usual and at the dinner she asked, as she often did, 'Where are ye working these days?'

He chewed and swallowed before answering. 'We're out in Portmarnock since Monday, finishing up that housing estate.'

'Oh. I thought I saw your van in Dorset Street on my way home. That mustn't have been you, so,' she said. She was afraid he might hear her heart pounding.

He shook his head. 'No, that wasn't me,' he said. 'I dropped Tony over to Swords on the way home.'

So much of the past made sense then. It was not his first time — there had been patterns: callers who hung up when she answered the phone, flurries of activity involving late evening jobs, sudden changes to his scheduled hours, weekend jobs to which he went off bright-eyed and happy, followed by months when there was no evening work, no weekend jobs, just evenings in, early nights and evasiveness. How blind she had been. She took a sip of water and looked at him. *Liar*, she thought, glaring at him and, for a second, there was panic in his eyes.

When bedtime came, she said, 'You can sleep in the front room from now on,' and there was no argument, no opposition, no discussion, ever.

That summer, she stared at dark-haired women on buses, or at any woman who walked slowly past her house or loitered near the library, any of whom might have been the choc-ice woman, coming to have a look at her. At lunchtime, she sat under a tree in the little park behind the library, and felt the world shrink to nothing but the terrible quivering of the birch leaves above her. She wrote letters to Frank that she never gave him. She thought herself a fool, a mug, a female cuckold; she thought the words 'unfaithful' and 'infidelity' – men's words – too tame, too benign. Call it what it is: *fornication.* She saw through walls into suburban houses, into the back of his van. She saw him arranging cushions and rugs, talking dirty, laughing, feasting on their bodies, cleaning up. The women would be coarse, sexually daring – devious even – and Frank would let that side of himself out. He would show them photographs and they would ridicule her. Yes, nunnish, they'd agree, a dry old stick, a prude. His was a sexless marriage, he'd tell them, and to top it all, she was barren. The mortification almost annihilated her. In her worst hours, she feared AIDS. Or a child. A child who would one day turn up on her doorstep to claim his inheritance. A child who would be legally entitled to part of her home. She lay awake at night, her mind lurching from one fear to the next. What if Frank fell in love with one of these women? What if he left her? What if *they* fell in love? What if they wanted rid of her? There was a murder case in the news at the time – a doctor and his lover were on trial for killing the woman's husband. Every night when the item came on the *Nine O'Clock* news, Frances could hardly breathe.

There were days when she felt she was walking through veils of fog, that reality was thin and provisional and at the same time terribly real and material and *fated.* She sensed danger everywhere. She moved carefully, holding on to handles and rails to anchor herself. She grew obsessive about hygiene, took copious showers, brutally scrubbed her body. At mealtimes, she could barely wait until Frank left the table before removing his plate and cup and cutlery, careful not to touch the handles, then wiping up every crumb, every atom of food he had dropped and which she had not taken her eyes off. She lost her appetite; certain foods – their textures and odours – repelled her. She saw sexual similes and correlations everywhere – she shunned milk first and then yogurt because they reminded her of semen. The revulsion spread to cheese and eggs, meats, animal fats. She grew thin and anxious and watchful, afraid that somehow her shame might be discernible. One Saturday morning, sitting at the kitchen table, she watched a truck park on the street outside her house, the livery of a tree surgeon company emblazoned on its side. A man and a boy of about twelve – the man's son, she guessed – set about their work, the father using a chainsaw to saw branches off a silver birch tree, the boy feeding the branches into the motorised shredder attached to the back of the truck. As she watched, she was lulled into a trance by the sounds and rhythm of their work – the revving of the chainsaw, the back-and-forth movement of man and boy, the groan of the shredder. The boy was bending and reaching and pushing. He stopped, then leaned in and tugged at a branch that was jammed in the shredder. He pushed the branch, and leaned in further and was swept from her view. Instantly a thick spray of blood and other material shot backwards and upwards into the air. The motor groaned and spluttered and ground to a halt. Everything grew still. She could not move. She sat in a daze, stupefied. And then, from the far side of the truck, the boy appeared, and behind him, his father. Still, she could not move. The man and the boy stood peering into the shredder, and then the man adjusted something in the machine, and the motor started up and they resumed their work. There were other hallucinatory moments. Late one night, in the middle of a film, the lead actress turned to Frances and addressed her directly through the TV screen. You must wash your tongue every night, she said. Frances knew it was all due to stress, stress and emotional overload.

The next day she would regain her equilibrium and tell herself she had overreacted, that she had exaggerated what she saw from the bus that evening, that there must be other explanations for the choc-ice woman. Because surely, *surely*, the housewives of Dublin were not so lustful that chance encounters with tradesmen led immediately to attacks of passion and fornication? And Frank was not a cruel or heartless man; he would never ridicule her, or harm her; he was incapable of doing evil. But in the evening, as the light faded, she'd remember the choc-ice woman again, the short dark hair, the bare, tanned arm. A nurse maybe, or a teacher, petite and pretty, and young, and Frances would feel sick and burdened all over again. She started checking the redial button on the phone late at night. Unfamiliar numbers occasionally appeared. One night she dialled, waited a few seconds after the woman answered. 'Listen,' she said, her calm voice belying the terror she felt. 'You're one of many. You're just one of his many whores.' She held her breath until the woman hung up. She did it again the following night. *Whore.*

The coffin was at the mouth of the hearse when she got back, resting waist-high on a stand, the lid unscrewed and sitting on top. As she approached, Mr O'Shea shook his head. 'I don't think it's him,' he said.

Frances shrugged. 'Not to worry. There's plenty of time to go back and get him.'

He slid the lid diagonally, and there was Denis, the flesh-coloured band still holding his mouth in place, the familiar collar of his pyjamas just visible below the zipped edges of the body bag.

She smiled and nodded. 'That's him, that's Denis.'

Mr O'Shea opened his mouth, then lowered his head and sighed. 'Thank God.'

She touched Denis's face. There was nothing of him left, nothing she might call a soul still lingering. Just this fast-disintegrating rag-tag of an old body, and her memories of him. She left her hand on his hair. Denis had been the lucky one. He had spent most of his life being tended to, sitting in his room reading, walking the fields on summer evenings. For as long as she remembered his life was entirely without conflict; he had not had to navigate ordinary human rela-tionships, or contend with the intense emotions and pain they bring. Whatever he had suffered in his youth, he had survived through the shelter of home. He had withdrawn from the world and turned inwards. Now she wonders if his youthful suffering had ever awoken an awareness of pain *outside* of himself, something greater than personal suffering. *She* has had intimations of pain outside of herself, moments when the whole suffering pantheon hits her: the poor, the sick, the homeless – all the suffering from time immemorial; the shackled slaves, the broken, the beaten, the abused; the raped, the pimped; and when a TV documentary on institutional child abuse came on, she would watch it for a few minutes and then switch channels or get up and put on a wash or clean out a cupboard, something to turn her own soul towards distraction.

'He doesn't look anywhere near seventy-six,' Mr O'Shea said.

'No, I suppose not. I forgot to say his hair was dark,' she said. 'He never went grey. It's no wonder you thought he was younger. My father was the same – people used to think he dyed it.'

When Mr O'Shea went to put the lid back on the coffin, she turned away. Suddenly she was alone in the world. From childhood came a prayer, unbidden, a chant she repeated in times of fear and danger. *Sacred Heart of Jesus, I place all my trust in thee.*

After he'd closed the hearse door, Mr O'Shea reached into his pocket. 'Do you mind if I smoke?'

She shook her head. 'I might join you.'

His hands shook slightly as he held his lighter to her cigarette. The first inhalation made her cough.

'You want to watch that cough!' he joked. He looked at his watch. 'Frank will get there well before us. Do you want to call him? He might be worried.'

'No, it's fine. He won't have long to wait.' She had switched off her phone before they arrived at the morgue this morning, to ensure nothing would intrude on her last day in Denis's presence.

'I'm Tom, by the way,' Mr O'Shea said, and proffered a hand.

After that first summer, she thought the worst was over. Then, one evening in late November, she was removing the day's newspapers from their station in the library when she spotted a headline in the health pages of the *Irish Times*. 'Chlamydia, the silent destroyer'. Her stomach lurched. She knew, before she read a word, what was in the article. She locked the library doors, switched off the main lights and sat at a low table in the children's corner. The complications listed – infertility, blocked fallopian tubes, ectopic pregnancy, miscarriage – had all been hers. She had always had an inkling, a vague sense of fear and foreboding around sex. She had put it down to the legacy of her upbringing, of being raised in an era when becoming pregnant outside marriage was the worst sentence a girl or woman could face – worse maybe than death. And as if that wasn't enough, the AIDS epidemic was at its height when Frances met Frank. It had not been easy at the start. Although Frank was gentle and kind, sex had been painful and messy and embarrassing. She had faulted herself, so she persevered and called down scenes from novels to aid arousal, and on those occasions when sex was pleasurable, she felt womanly and worldly and sophisticated, like a character in a film. But the unease and the sense of foreboding were never far off. Now, it was almost a relief to know that they had not come from nothing.

Back on the road, Mr O'Shea was in a grateful, almost buoyant mood.

'You know we always check that we're picking up the right sex — when we're collecting remains, I mean. Make sure it's a man if it's a man you're supposed to be collecting. Or — well, thank God it's rare that you'd be collecting a child. But lord God, no way does your brother look his age. He could easily pass for forty with that head of black hair.'

She never confronted Frank. Instead, on quiet mornings in the library, she went online and read about the bacterium she had unwittingly hosted in her body for years. *Chlamydia trachomatis*, derived from the Greek word for cloak, may have originated in amphibians, most likely frogs. She pored over the microscopic images on the screen, magnified into bulging, purple, misshapen globules, and thought of them invading and contaminating the pink flesh of her cervix and womb and fallopian tubes. Thus began a deeper loathing of Frank. She began to detest his bodily presence, his smell, the sound of his chewing. In the evenings, they ate in silence. When Frank moved to clear the dishes — or do any task in the kitchen — she lifted her hand, 'Leave that, I'll do it,' and meekly he acquiesced. He could have left. She could have asked him to leave, she could have screamed, *Go on, get out! Go to one of your fancy women.* But she was not a screamer any more than

100

he was. Eventually, she summoned the courage to see an STI consultant in a private clinic, and told the woman the whole story. A week later, the tests came back positive for chlamydia, negative for everything else. How could she have recognised the symptoms? she pleaded. She had been a virgin, a novice on her wedding night. She had assumed the pain and discomfort and discharge were associated with intercourse, having nothing else to compare them with. Sitting there in the privacy of the doctor's office, Frances started to cry for the fool of a woman she had been. She went home, started a course of antibiotics and went to bed for the weekend, full of hatred for Frank and for her own befouled body.

There was a Robert Musil story that Frances came upon around that time. The protagonist, a student of chemistry and technology, became involved with Tonka, a humble, passive girl who had been hired to care for his grandmother. He believed he'd once caught sight of her in the countryside, standing outside a cottage. His friend told him that hundreds of such girls laboured in the fields when the beet was being harvested and they were as submissive as slaves to their supervisors. The young man saw something noble in this simple creature, in her natural helplessness. He thought: if it were not for him, who would understand her? When his grandmother died, he took Tonka away with him to Berlin. He did not love her, exactly, but he saw her as pure and natural and unspoilt. He loved all her little defects, even her deformed fingernail, the result of a work injury. He believed she rinsed his soul clean. After some years Tonka became pregnant. The dates revealed that he was away on a journey at the time of conception, but Tonka had no memory of anything having happened, and there was no other man he could suspect. Wilfully blind, he began to wonder if it could have been an immaculate conception. Then Tonka became ill with a horrible, dangerous, 'insidious' infection – syphilis. His doctors found no trace of the disease in him, and his mother hinted that Tonka was a prostitute. He grew suspicious and superstitious and tried to get Tonka to confess, but she was steadfast in her denials. Send me away if you won't believe me, she said calmly. He sought several doctors' opinions, hoping for a rational explanation that would prove she was innocent. He wrestled with philosophical and scientific questions, like the fact that one has to believe *in* a thing – a chair, a table – before the thing could exist before one's eyes. His private ordeal revolved around this question of belief – could he force himself to believe in Tonka's innocence despite the overwhelming evidence that she had been unfaithful? The disease progressed and Tonka grew sick and gaunt and ugly, but he cared for her and nursed her, all the time wavering between hope and despair. He believed that despite Tonka's outwardly ugliness, inwardly she was pure and of deep significance, and her goodness was mysterious, like a dog's goodness. And then one day, Tonka's old calendar lay open and the young man saw, among other domestic entries, a little red exclamation mark that recorded the incident that Tonka denied. Frances remembered the young man's mental anguish, how demented he was with dreams and visions, and feelings that were constantly oscillating. He did not believe Tonka, but he believed *in* Tonka. After her death he had a clear conscience and was sure that because of her, because her small, warm shadow had fallen across his life, he was a better person.

When she first read the story, Frances had kept waiting for the child to be born to Tonka, but it was never mentioned. She found herself constantly thinking about the story, slipping into the pallid, shadowy realm that the protagonist inhabited. In that kind of daydreaming state, she experienced a floating sense of calm. It was not that she was briefly happy or more content, but that she existed at a deeper level than in her daily waking life.

They were on the ring road around Limerick city. Mr O'Shea was tapping lightly on the steering wheel.

'We'll be home in good time after all,' he said. 'Frank won't have too long to wait.'

'No,' she said.

After a few moments, he gave her an inquisitive look. 'Frank isn't a Kerry man, is he?'

'No. Kilkenny.'

Over the years, much of the pain had abated. Little things had helped. The habit of passing the women's prison every morning on her way to work and imagining the lives behind the walls; women driven to kill their men after years of being kicked and beaten, of losing their minds and their pregnancies. There were worse fates than hers, she knew. Frank had not a violent bone in his body; he was soft and slow and gentle. As he aged, he had put on weight, and walked with a slow, lumbering gait that reminded her of a toddler's waddle. She would catch sight of him bending down to tie a shoelace or putting on his jacket in the hall, and something about the lonely slope of his shoulders would soften her and remind her of the boy he had been. Then she would catch herself. *Beware of pity, Frances.*

She glanced at her watch. By now, Frank would be parked outside the funeral home waiting for them, worried by their delay. She had lied to the STI doctor. When the doctor said that Frank would have to be told, and treated for chlamydia, Frances had nodded. But she had no intention of telling him. Let him go on infecting them, she thought. Let them rot, and let the nasty little bacterium keep gnawing away at him too.

She turned to Mr O'Shea.

'My husband is a serial adulterer,' she announced. She had been rehearsing those words in her head for years.

Mr O'Shea looked at her in panic, briefly tripped up, she could tell, by that word 'serial'. Then he gave a little cough, and cleared his throat. 'I'm very sorry,' he said. 'That's terrible. I don't know what to say.'

He looked at her softly, pitifully, and for an instant she was afraid he might put his hand on hers. She looked out her window. Maybe you're one too, she thought. If I were a different woman, younger, more attractive – or maybe not even attractive, but capable of giving off a certain signal – would he be game too? If I indicated availability and secreted the right pheromones, he might at any minute exit

the motorway, drive down a forest track or quiet lane —
because he would know all the forest tracks and quiet lanes
— and there might be some talk or laughter, and maybe even
a little awkwardness as he unbuckled, and then he would
do it and I would let him, with my dead brother lying there,
inches from our heads.

Dusk was falling as they crossed the county boundary into
Kerry. She had the feeling that they had travelled on high
ground or crossed mountains and were now descending into
a valley. The last of the evening light appeared between the
clouds, signalling, she thought, winter's end. She wondered
what angle she will have on her life, her whole existence,
when the end approaches. And what angle will Frank have
on his life, if he ever ponders such things? He is not the
kind who acknowledges events or experiences or gives weight
or meaning to them. He might have regarded the infidelities
and the individual women themselves as he regards his
breakfast or his dinner, or his daily work — something to
be attended to at that moment, but something to be gotten
through nonetheless. It is difficult to know what, if anything,
has meaning for Frank. If she has meaning for him. She
knows precisely what meaning Frank has for her — he is a
weight that will never leave her. They are bound together
under one roof. She has been exiled with him within the
walls of her childhood home. They will grow old and infirm
together. She will tend to his body, or he to hers, and it
will start tomorrow, or the next day. In time, memory will
fade and with it certain images. The small boy creeping out

at night to retrieve a sweet from the floor of a tractor will fade. Instead, it will be Frank as he is today or will be tomorrow, standing behind the cowshed, sucking the sweet slowly until the chocolate is gone and the desiccated coconut forms a hard, tight little ball in his mouth.

The streetlights were on when they arrived in Castleisland. They turned off Main Street. Frank was parked across from the funeral home. The sight of his broad outline in the darkness brought a feeling of lonely but familiar comfort. She did not know what Frank wanted. She had never known. In their life together, she had made all the decisions. She had brought them to Kerry without consideration for him. He had objected to nothing and she had taken his silence as acquiescence. And what of his suffering? Where had he put the lost mother, the abandoned child and all the sad days that followed? Had he reined it all in, sublimated everything? Everything except the sex.

Mr O'Shea drove around the back of his premises and parked the hearse in an empty yard and turned off the engine. For a moment, all was darkness. Then a light came on and a door opened. And from around the side of the building, Frank's outline appeared. As he approached, he seemed not to get any closer. She squinted in the twilight. Any moment now, she thought, I will be able to make out his face. As she waited, a question rose. Who is the choc-ice woman? The choc-ice woman is nobody. Then Tonka came to mind, and with her the warm familiarity that her story always brought. Tonka, gaunt and ugly on her deathbed, with her secret locked inside her. And the young man, who had loved her deformed fingernail, crying out her name and understanding, for an instant, all he had never understood, and feeling her, from the ground under his feet to the top of his head, feeling the whole of her life, in him.

Assignation

At seven-thirty Marion wakes the little girl, helps her get dressed and leads her downstairs for breakfast. Afterwards, she puts on the child's coat and hat, then her own, and they walk four blocks along Broadway to the school. It is a bright morning in mid April. Already Marion can feel the warmth, the change in the seasons. She holds the little girl's hand and steers her along the pavement through the morning crowds – men in suits and hats hurrying to work, delivery boys on bicycles, street vendors, gangs of schoolboys. This is Elizabeth's first day back at school after a brief illness, and she can sense the uncertainty in the grip of the child's hand and the way she looks up at Marion and waits for the nod before they cross the street. But for the difference in eye colour and Marion's plain wool coat and worn leather boots, she might be mistaken for the child's mother.

All morning she goes about her duties. She strips the beds and takes the dirty linen and laundry from the bedroom hampers down to the basement and loads the rotary tub, then switches the machine on. She keeps Elizabeth's clothes separate from the adult clothes, occasionally washing them by hand in the zinc tub, taking extra care with the little dresses and blouses and underwear.

This is her third spring in the country, her third year in the employment of the Cooke family. She knows now what lies ahead from day to day and week to week: the house-work, the care of Elizabeth, the grocery shopping, the errands she runs for Mrs Cooke. She has one afternoon off each week, usually on a Wednesday, during which she wanders around Greenwich Village, alone or with her friend Lizzie Burke from Sligo or other Irish girls she has come to know, stopping to buy pretzels or roast chickpeas from a street vendor, or trawling through small stores for trinkets. In Woolworths, she buys hand lotion and nail polish, and often comes on items — colouring pencils, ribbons, tiny porcelain animals — that would make nice presents for Elizabeth. Only once did she succumb and buy a furry green-and-black caterpillar that Elizabeth holds when Marion takes her on her lap and reads to her in the play-room each evening.

At ten-thirty, she knocks gently on the study door. Mrs Cooke, seated at her bureau, turns slightly in her chair. 'I'm almost done, Marion,' she says. 'Come on in.'

Even now, she is still sometimes taken aback when she hears her name. On the ship over from Ireland she had met another Mayo girl, also named Mary, who was going to an aunt in Boston. The girl's aunt had instructed her to change her name to Marion, because there are too many Marys in America now.

Mrs Cooke is folding a sheet of cream notepaper, placing it inside an envelope. 'How was Elizabeth this morning?'

'Very well, Mrs Cooke. Happy to be going back to school.'

'Poor sweetie.'

Mrs Cooke's hands are smooth and creamy, unmarked by labour. Her fingers have acquired a sheen from the touch of beautiful things: silk, linen, fine notepaper. Her name, Edith, and that of her husband, William Cooke, are inscribed in gold lettering on the top left-hand corner of each sheet of notepaper, followed by their address and telephone number. Every morning, Mrs Cooke attends to her mail and her diary appointments, and on days when they are hosting dinner, she works on the menu. Mr Cooke is an attorney and they frequently have esteemed people, men mostly, to dinner. President Roosevelt is a former client of his firm. Mrs Cooke's father is a former governor of Connecticut. Mrs Cooke herself is a member of several clubs and charities – the Ladies' Aid Society, a bridge club, a flower-arranging club. She volunteers at a soup kitchen every Friday.

Now, turning slightly in her chair, Mrs Cooke hands Marion the letters for posting.

'Thank you, dear,' she says. 'Oh, you remember Walter will be home tomorrow, don't you?'

'Yes, Mrs Cooke, his room is ready.'

Walter is sixteen and will be home from his school in Massachusetts for Easter vacation. It is expected that he will follow in his father's footsteps and enter Harvard Law School.

Mrs Cooke tilts her head. 'It's this afternoon you're taking off, isn't it, Marion?'

'Yes, ma'am. If that is still all right.'

'Of course. Do you have something special planned?'

'I'm just . . . No, Mrs Cooke. Nothing special.'

'Well, you have a nice time. I'm going to take Elizabeth up to Macy's for some new summer dresses. And you'll be back for her bedtime. The President is delivering another fireside chat on the radio this evening, so Mr Cooke and I will say goodnight to her a little earlier than usual.'

Hannah, the housekeeper-cook, is seated at the kitchen table writing the shopping list. She is a tall, thin woman with strands of grey running through her dark hair. Behind her, gleaming copper pots and pans hang from hooks above the stove, and enamel containers and glass jars with flour, sugar, spices sit on the open shelves. On other shelves and inside cabinets there is an array of bowls, chinaware, blue and amber pitchers, Venetian glass flasks for vinegar and oil, serving platters, tureens, silver domed warmers. In Marion's first weeks here, Hannah seemed stern and forbidding, but she proved to be a calm and patient teacher. She taught Marion how to prepare vegetables, make stock, set the table. She encouraged her to write down the new words – applesauce, cantaloupe, jellied fruit, pickled beets – and the ingredients of each dish. She learned that oysters are served raw and lemon pudding is decorated with shards of green angelica.

Hannah is originally from Belfast and has been with the Cooke family for twenty-six years. She is Presbyterian, and goes to church with the Cookes on Sunday mornings and teases Marion about being a Papist. She told Marion she was terrified of Catholics when she was a child. She used to hurry past the high wall of the convent in Belfast in case a nun would jump out and grab her and pull her inside. She has never been back home, but she tells Marion about her family. Under her bed, she keeps a box with envelopes which contain human hair – strands of her dead father's and mother's hair, a lock of her dead little brother's taken before the lid was placed on his coffin. Marion got a shock at the sight of the hair – some of it almost fifty years old.

Before the stock market crashed eight years ago, the Cooke family had a butler, an upstairs maid and a chauffeur-cum-handyman, as well as Hannah. For a while after Elizabeth was born, there had been a nursemaid and then, when she was four, Marion arrived. She took to the Cooke family immediately. Everything – this whole civilised life – had cast its spell on her: the elegant rooms, the angelic child, the endearments spoken by the husband to the wife, *darling* and *dearest*. She began to emulate Mrs Cooke's poise and mannerisms. She held her back and shoulders straight when she walked; she bathed regularly, took care of her hands, carefully laundered her clothes. Caring for Elizabeth, as it turned out, had been not like work at all. One day while

Marion was ironing Elizabeth's clothes, Hannah stopped talking suddenly and, without removing her eyes from the task she was doing, said, 'Don't you get too attached to that child.'

She walks three blocks to the grocery store on 18th Street, stopping at a mailbox on a corner to post the letters. Alone, now, a slight anxiety enters her. On the pavement men and women walk by, and occasionally a man's eyes meet hers and, briefly, something – a flicker of something – passes between them that shames and frightens her. She slips her right hand inside her coat, furtively, and reaches under her left arm until her fingertips find the familiar indent in her armpit through the fabric of her dress. She rests her fingers there for a moment, relieved, and then withdraws them.

This afternoon she is going on an assignation. That is what Lizzie Burke called it. She is to meet Lizzie's cousin, Michael Lawlor, in Washington Square Park at four p.m. They met once before outside St Joseph's Church after Mass one Sunday morning. He kept his hands in his pockets when Lizzie introduced them. His hair was jet black and perhaps his eyes were brown and he had a bashful look. But a few minutes later, after they had moved away from each other and their eyes met, he smiled, and he did not seem bashful at all, but eager and open and hopeful. A week later, he wrote Lizzie a letter asking if she, Marion, was already spoken for.

She waits in line in the grocery store and hands her list

to the storekeeper. She nods to another housemaid she recognises from 23rd Street. Back on the street, she passes three small boys playing marbles. Suddenly she pictures Elizabeth at her desk in school. She will be listening out for the bell, for class to end. She begins to hurry. Last night she dreamt her mother had gone up a steep hill and tripped on her long dress and broken her leg. In the morning she thought it was true. She reached inside her nightdress, touched the familiar little hollow in her armpit, closed her eyes. 'Take your hand out of there,' her mother said to her crossly. She was back in childhood, and it was bedtime and her mother lifted her arm and looked silently, solemnly, into her armpit.

'Why have I a hole there?' she asked. Her mother looked away.

'Stop calling it a hole,' she snapped. 'It's all healed up, so it's not a hole.'

'But why have I it?'

Her mother was annoyed, then she sighed. 'It was a boil you got when you were a baby, and it festered. It was my fault. It was an awful hot summer the year you were born, and I should have changed your vest and washed you more often. You were crying and crying and I didn't know what was wrong with you.' Her mother was nearly crying now. 'In the end Nurse Brown had to come and lance it. It'll go away, though, it'll close up, I promise. Come on, get into bed now. It'll be better before you get married.'

It is what adults say to children at home when they fall

and hurt themselves. She says it to Elizabeth when the child takes a tumble or scratches or grazes herself. Don't worry, sweetheart, it'll be better before you get married.

After lunch, Mrs Cooke goes out and Marion attends to the first-floor rooms. She moves around the drawing room, then the dining room, dusting, polishing, plumping up cushions, fixing the long silk drapes in their ties. She inhales the spicy smell of mahogany and is caught off guard by the beautiful tinkle of crystal glasses when they accidentally touch, and then, when she turns around, by the sunlight falling on the rug at her feet. She is touched by the stillness in each room, by the order and harmony – the candles standing straight in their candlesticks, the tablecloths folded inside drawers lined with green baize. She treads softly and breathes lightly so as not to trespass upon this peace. Someday, she thinks, I will have my own rooms. She pauses, listens to the clock ticking, the rustle – she is certain there is a rustle – among the folds of the drapes. She can feel the eyes of Mr Cooke's male ancestors looking down at her from the walls. Everything watching her, as much as she watches everything from the corner of her eye or the back of her head. Everything on the point of movement, ready to shift or stir and come to life – a twitch of an ancestor's moustache, a fluttering in the trailing ivy on the wallpaper, the sigh of a spoon as it nestles against its neighbour inside the canteen of cutlery in a drawer. She is not afraid that such things might happen. She understands it is possible, but she senses something serene and docile and benevolent in these rooms, and when she gently closes a drawer and confines its contents to darkness and turns to leave the room, she has a longing to say something, to offer comfort, to whisper, 'There, there . . . I'll be back.'

At two p.m. she is walking through Washington Square Park with Elizabeth, on their way home from school, the child's hand in hers. The path is strewn with blooms from pink cherry blossoms, like snow at their feet. They stand for a while at the fountain. Elizabeth is a quiet child who rarely, even when asked, shares news or events from her school day. They pass an old lady on a bench, with a small white dog on a sheepskin rug beside her. The thought comes to Marion as they stroll along the path with the small birds at their feet, how beautiful the world is. They find a vacant bench and sit. She remembers Michael Lawlor's face from that Sunday morning outside the church. She has had moments, little visions, when she imagines she is walking along the street beside him, his reassuring presence reminding her of the feeling she'd had walking down the street in Westport with her father and her brother Mossie, the way she'd felt enveloped in their warmth and protection, the smell of tobacco, their manly certainties. In her visions of herself and Michael Lawlor there are, sometimes, children.

After a while Elizabeth turns to her. 'Tell me about the day your papa left the barn door open,' she says.

She has told the child stories about home and her own childhood, about her sister Eileen, who is the same age as Elizabeth, and Maureen, who is eighteen, and the twins who are fourteen; about the fields and the sheep, the lane down to the shore. 'And the fool of a dog,' Elizabeth reminds her often. 'Don't forget that fool of a dog.' The more stories of home she tells the child, the further that life removes itself from her and becomes someone else's.

'One day my father left the barn door open,' she starts. 'And the horse got out and trampled on the bicycle in the yard. My mother had no bicycle to go to Westport on after that.'

'And she grew very quiet,' Elizabeth says.

'She did . . . She grew very quiet.'

Occasionally, when the wind rises and gulls circle over the streets, she thinks she can smell sea air, and in that moment she has an intimation of home, of the silvery waters of the bay, of her mother lifting a pot off the fire and turning her face towards the window light. They will have forgotten her by now, their days too filled with work and weather, with cows to be milked, crops to be sown, to indulge in the luxury of remembrance.

A pigeon hops into view, and then a candy wrapper blows along the path and comes to rest before them. Elizabeth is watching it too, but she does not stir. She does not look at Marion or point to it or break the silence. She has a way of getting down under things, a way of following Marion's mind too, sensing her faint, soft thoughts as they form. Marion thinks of Elizabeth's nature as pure and sublime, and she, Marion, its guardian, and she is sure that from such nature will grow tender feeling and a refined soul. Sometimes, on the street, they pass strikers carrying placards or a line of men at a soup kitchen, or a gang of roving boys or a paperboy, thin and hungry, calling out in a raucous voice, and she can feel the tug in Elizabeth's hand as she slows and stares, and Marion watches her and sees the child grow thoughtful, sees what she is seeing, and lets her see. They have been separated just once, when the family went to visit Mrs Cooke's relations in Connecticut for three weeks last summer. To be parted from the child for one day is hard to bear, let alone twenty-two.

Finally, the hour has come. Her good navy dress is draped on the back of the chair. She sits on the edge of her bed and looks around the small room, at the patch of sky beyond the window. Her room is high up under the eaves and in summer it becomes unbearable hot. That first year, she used to lie awake at night with the window open, listening to sounds in the distance. Men coming home from the bars, laughter, curses, cries in the night air. Sometimes brawling. Women too. She was too high up to make out the words. She often lay awake until dawn, and then got up and watched the sun rising over the rooftops. It was at dawn she thought most about home, the sun setting on the water, the whole length of the horizon in the distance.

The day before she left home, she and Eileen – and the fool of a dog – crossed the strand to the little island of Inistubbrid. They walked up the lane to the ruins of their grandparents' house, and they counted the sheep and then sat quietly on the grass, pulling daisies and hardly speaking. That night, the house filled up with neighbours, relations, the priest too. They all came with good wishes, and some pressed money into Marion's hand. She sat on a chair beside her mother for a long time. Then she helped Maureen serve the tea and sandwiches and whiskey. The singing and dancing went on until the early hours. Originally, it was Mossie who was to come out, but when the time came to book the ticket her father could not bear to let him go. Mary can go instead, he said.

In her letters home, she has never told them that she changed her name. She reaches under her bed now and pulls out a shoebox with her mother's letters, and reads the first one that was waiting for her when she arrived in New York.

My Dear Mary,

You are halfway out by this. Oh I wish this week was over. I have a bad feeling. I am wondering are you sick. Mossie is very lonely for you, and the twins and Eileen too. She cried all day after you left. Mossie didn't get out of the bed on Saturday. Another crowd came on Friday night and we were worn out. They meant well. Well Mary three days are gone now but it seems like a year. They were all coming up to me after Mass yesterday. Sr. Concepta said the nuns are praying for your safe voyage. I wasn't in Westport since. I sent Maureen in to sell the eggs on Saturday. Seán cut a bit of the hedge today and your father sold sheep at the fair in Newport and brought home ice cream. Maureen is helping me a lot. I hate to come into the house when there's no one here. I'll go to bed now Mary and I'll write again in the morning before I post this.

This is Tuesday. I hope you aren't sick. I forgot to tell you the Durkans were disappointed you didn't call to say goodbye. I wish it was Friday and I wouldn't have to wait for the post but then I'd be wishing it was Monday. Will you write a long letter to me. And mind yourself and be good to everyone you meet. And say your prayers.

God bless, Mama.

Her hands are trembling. She need not go at all. She can, if she wishes, simply go down two flights of stairs and wait in the playroom for Elizabeth's return. Later she can help with her schoolwork, read from her book about star constellations. Pegasus. Sirius. The Plough. She has often searched the night sky for these constellations, but has never found any. It is because of the city lights. They would have been easy to find in the sky above Mayo, if only she had known of their existence then.

She glances at the clock. She thought he had a kind face that morning outside the church, and kind eyes. Lizzie had done most of the talking. He had only come out a few weeks beforehand. She remembered her own first weeks, and felt a great surge of pity for him.

'He has a good job, a good wage,' Lizzie had said when she told Marion about the letter from Michael. 'He's a longshoreman — that means he works in the docks, unloading ships.'

'I know what it means,' she said.

She gets up and puts on the dress. She stands before the mirror and pulls her hair back and practises a smile. She starts to rehearse a question. Her heart thumps hard and she turns from the mirror quickly, and automatically reaches inside her dress and lets her fingers probe her armpit for one last reassuring touch. As she withdraws her hand, she is caught by a wave of sorrow.

In those first days last summer when Elizabeth was in Connecticut, Marion had found it hard to rise in the mornings. She lay listening to footsteps on the sidewalk, cars in the distance. She tried to imagine Connecticut. A big house with a lawn and cars parked on a gravel drive, cousins, a grandmother. With the child absent and her chores done, the afternoons stretched before her, empty. Her limbs grew slow and heavy in the heat, and one afternoon she went down to Elizabeth's room and lay on her bed. As she dozed off to sleep she looked up and saw her own mother's photograph on the chest of drawers. What if I die here? she thought. She had not seen any graveyards other than very old churchyards with a few ancient tombstones behind locked gates. When she woke up there was, of course, no photograph.

The arrangement is that she will meet him at the east entrance to Washington Square Park. She walks past the arch with the traffic passing underneath. Above the din, a paperboy is calling out the latest news headlines. Along the path, a little swarm of robins rises suddenly from a tree. Further on, a preacher is standing on a wooden box calling out to the tramps gathered round, eager to save their souls. Repent! She stands and listens for a moment, reminded of the priests who came to the parish every second year for the Mission.

The blood is thumping in her temples, and the sun is starting to give her a headache. She moves into the shade. Involuntarily, her right hand reaches inside her coat and then, remembering where she is, she quickly withdraws it. She rounds the corner and slows her step. She is about forty yards from the east entrance. She can see people entering and leaving, and others standing around waiting. She stops and stands under a tree.

He is there. Tall, black-haired, in a dark-grey jacket; she recognises his profile. He glances furtively at the faces that pass. He turns and shows his face and she pulls back into the shadows. He takes out a cigarette and strikes a match, brings his hands to his face. As the smoke curls out of his mouth she realises that the time has arrived. Thoughts rise and collide with each other. And then older, half-forgotten thoughts and memories arrive and collide with the new thoughts until she feels sick and dizzy. She leaves a hand on the railing to steady herself, but she cannot stop this splitting and mixing of memories with reality, and for a moment she sees Elizabeth on a headland dotted with sheep and her grandparents' house with the roof fallen in and her mother throwing her head back, laughing, and all of them going to Mass in Newport on Easter Sunday morning. Summer evenings there, and here too, the sky streaked with pink at sunset. Life, and the evening, almost too beautiful to bear. All these things now colliding inside her, confusing her, and the sun too, blinding her, giving her a splitting headache, so that she cannot think straight, cannot think what to do, or how to be, or who she belongs to.

She had gone outside that night before she left home, to gather her thoughts and escape the music and laughter and the intense scrutiny of others. It was around midnight, a warm summer's night. At the gable end of the house, a few neighbouring men stood talking and smoking. The O'Malley brothers, from the other end of the village, were there. Tom, the older one, was about Mossie's age, and Liam was her own age. She smiled as she went past. She opened the gate to the pony's paddock and entered and walked along the stone wall until the sounds of the music and the voices back at the house grew faint. The moon was out. She could hear the sea in the distance. She would never again have a daylight view out onto the bay, or of the islands lying out there like resting giants. She walked along the wall to the place where the shore came into view, and stood looking down at the waves lapping.

And then she felt a presence behind her, and when she turned the two O'Malley brothers were there. Startled, she greeted them uncertainly, and smiled weakly. Something about them – their silence, the way they had crept up on her – unnerved her. Neither of them answered her greeting. Tom stepped closer and said her name, *Mary Joyce*, in a mocking voice. He put his hand on her arm. Confused, she stared at his hand and was still staring at it when Liam stepped forward on the other side of her. 'I've to go in now,' she said, and she went to move. But they blocked her way, first to the right and then to the left, and when she tried again they grabbed her by the arms. She tried to turn and free herself, but their bodies were hard against her, like a wall. She drew her right foot back to kick them, but her long skirt prevented her from raising her leg. Suddenly her right hand was free, and she lashed out and scratched one of them in the face. Then, abruptly, she was pushed to the ground, face down, hands held behind her back.

She heard laughter, and remembered the men at the gable end of the house, and called out for help. They were pulling off her stockings, her undergarments. Stop, stop it, she was crying. Please, she begged. A stone lay to the right, inches from her face. If she could free her hand.

Then one of them spoke. 'You go first.'

With sudden force, and in one swift movement, she was pitched over onto her back. The sound of a belt buckle, the flash of white skin in the moonlight. She tried to kick her legs free. Then she paused, lifted her head a little.

'I'll tell on ye,' she said coldly.

A chuckle from deep in the throat of the one holding her down. 'Who'll you tell? You're going to America in the morning, and you won't be back.'

Later, when the second one was at her, she heard the waves on the other side of the wall breaking on the shore, and she had a clear image of the tide edging up along the sand, closer and closer, so close that the waves might break over the wall and reach her head and her body, her hair, and into her parched mouth would flow the salty water.

*   *   *

This is her chance. Michael Lawlor might be her only chance. But what does she know of him? She does not know if he is cruel or kind, or soft, or manly. She knows nothing of his private life, or the private life of any man. She takes a deep breath. He is, from what she knows, a good man. She will have a home, children. She will have fine rugs and velvet curtains. But how to get to that point, how to know what to do now, this minute. How to know what to say, when to smile, how to hide the shame. *Because he will know.* A man will know. He will see something in her eyes, and know. And if he does not know now, he will know later. On the wedding night, a man would be able to tell.

Slowly, she stirs and leans out of her hiding place. He is still there, by the entrance, pacing back and forth. Suddenly he walks out the gate, leaves the park. Her stomach lurches. But, almost immediately, he returns and starts to walk away in the other direction.

She begins to follow. He turns onto the south path. She keeps well back, close to the trees. His head turns slightly to the right or left as young women approach. He turns onto the west side. All her attention is on his back, on the grey jacket. He turns right onto the north side of the park, and she follows him until he has circled the whole park and he is back again at the east entrance. He stands and turns his head to give one last look, and for a second she freezes and thinks he has seen her. But his eyes glide past her and his whole body turns, and he walks away.

She leaves by the north entrance and walks up Broadway. Elizabeth and her mother will be finished in Macy's now.

They will have taken the elevator down from the children's department with their purchases — little dresses wrapped in tissue paper — in beribboned boxes. Afterwards, they might go to Schrafft's for ice-cream sundaes. She wanders around the streets for a long time. She will be paid on Friday. She will go to Schrafft's herself some Wednesday afternoon. She thinks it is better to be free and independent. She thinks of the evening ahead, the playroom, the constellations book in her hands. She had arrived into this family three years ago, and in the child's presence she had felt absolved. She turns, walks back along Broadway. In a few hours they will be home. She quickens her step and her heart begins to quell. There is, she thinks, something in life after all.

The Hitchhiker

For three hours they drove east without talking. The sun lit up the bare trees on the road ahead. They passed small deserted villages, downcast and desolate after the winter. She looked out the window at a house or a garden or a tree, turning her head slowly and deliberately, indicating some proud implacable stance. When he changed gears, his arm brushed hers. A delicate silence hung between them, neither ceding to be the first to speak. In certain moments, however, in a yawn or a sigh, in the little concessional noises he made, she sensed something infinitely tender in him. It would not take much, perhaps a thought, for one of them to make an offering.

She remembered other journeys, travelling in the confined space of the car, when the hum of the engine led each of them to distant, vaguely happy thoughts, before the city lights brought them to their senses again. She thought of them as permanently in transit, forever journeying together like this. Years ago, just after they met, she had had to drive to Cork and back in a day, and he had come along on a whim. She had driven more slowly than usual, to stretch out time. She knew that the moment he left the car all the goodness of her life would go with him. She resented stopping off to eat, or sharing him with others in a public place. He crowded her thoughts, and she was alert to every breath, every tensing muscle, every minute gesture. She was given over completely, soft and yielding on the outside, tense, febrile, consumed within. His hands rested calmly on his thighs that day, proud, indifferent; he would not give. She thought him impervious, untouched by the pitch and charge of feeling in the car. Towards the end of the journey, she looked in the rear-view mirror and saw the long line of road disappear behind her, and somehow the agitation abated and something passed between them, as if they had found the hidden parts of each other. She looked out at the trees against the sky, and she knew then her fate with him was sealed. She longed to mark the moment, take his hand, leave it on her lap, make something of it.

Outside, now, the small farms and stone walls of the west gave way to open fields and occasional groves of trees. He picked up speed on the open road through the midlands. She turned her head to look at him. It seemed that everything she knew or had ever known was within him, or had come out of him, or been deemed by him.

It was April, and they had rented an island cottage at the edge of the Atlantic where the sharp white light and the waves and surf surrounded them. The island was in his blood; he knew its paths and its people. In the mornings he rose early from the bed and she rolled over into his space and listened for sounds – the kettle boiling, the time signal on the radio, the clatter of delft – in the kitchen. She heard him slip out of the cottage, his footsteps trailing away. She lay very still then, waiting for his return, to feel herself reconstituted again.

One morning she stood at the bedroom window and watched him on the strand below. He was looking out to sea as the surf washed over his shoes. How small and mortal he looked before the waves, with the sands darkening around him. She thought he might be drawn in by the dark undertow. She always feared losing him. Still sleepy, she strained to reach him across the cold air.

'Did you get up last night?' he asked at breakfast. 'I thought I felt you getting up.'

She shook her head.

He stopped stirring his coffee. 'What?' he asked. 'What are you thinking?'

'Nothing,' she said.

She had woken at dawn, exhausted and unnerved by the subterranean pull of her sleep. She slipped from the bed and put on her coat and went outside. She crossed the rough grass behind the cottage and rested against a rock. The horizon was streaked with pink as the sun broke through. Her shoes were wet from the dew. She had the feeling of being watched, but when she looked back at the bedroom window he was not there. She turned to her left and there, a few feet away, stood a fox, silent and motionless. Her heart froze. His body was old and worn and wretched. The sun's rays pierced his irises. A flicker of recognition passed between them, and she saw suffering in his eyes and she had the feeling that they had been standing there together since the beginning of time. She could hear the lapping of the waves behind her. Then the fox turned away and disappeared through the hedge.

'I must have been dreaming,' he said. 'I was sure you were gone from the bed for a while.'

On their last day they walked around the island, weaving their way in and out of tiny beaches and around headlands. Small, bleached bones lay on the sand, and he kicked one and kept walking and then scaled a low cliff. The gulls circled and screeched overhead. They came upon bunches of primroses and she plucked some and held them up to him and told him of the May altars she'd made as a child. They followed a path along the headland, and she turned and stood for a moment. She saw his eyes linger on the cliffs, the waves, the islands in the distance. She thought he must be thinking that this was the view his antecedents had had for hundreds of years, that nothing had changed.

They hung on to each other that evening. He cooked dinner and she sat reading by the fire in the next room. She heard his movements in the kitchen, and the tinkle of lids and the rush of tap water. The radio played traditional music. He would be standing beside steaming saucepans, a fork in his hand, reel music in his head, poised to test the potatoes. He kept coming into the room, his sleeves rolled, setting the table, opening the wine, checking the weather and the waves beyond the window. Given up to each task. Humming softly, thinking himself alone.

When they sat down to eat, he touched her elbow and said, 'Go ahead, start.' They talked a little of the day. The music streamed in from the kitchen, and she saw how the notes and the wine and the dying light softened him. Afterwards, she returned to her book. He remained at the table with a local newspaper spread out before him. Time passed and when she remembered him and looked up she was surprised, elated, he was still there.

'Tell me,' she said, 'about the others, before me. Before you met me.'

He looked up, a little dazed.

'Why?' His voice was hoarse and remote.

She shrugged and smiled. She was a little drunk.

'There's nothing to tell,' he said, shaking his head.

'Please. Tell me. Tell me about . . . Ann or Catherine or Ruth. Tell me about Ruth.'

'It was years ago. I forget all that, it's of no consequence.' He gestured with open hands. 'This, the here and now – this is what counts.'

'You couldn't forget. People don't – they never forget things like that. They're too private.'

'Leave them, then.'

His eyes were wide and those words, 'Leave them then', disquieted her. 'I want to know,' she pressed.

He rose and went into the kitchen. It was dusk then and the ocean seemed far off. He had said that name, Ruth, in his sleep in their early days and it had remained a faint, abstract pain in a distant part of her. She was not privy to all of him.

'Okay then,' he said, when he returned.

She closed her book. She could barely make out his face. Suddenly she knew why she did this, why she pushed him to reveal his life before her. She wanted to map him, decipher him, turn over every inch of him, every disparate clue, and find the cause of him. Know the absoluteness of him.

'I was young, only twenty or twenty-one, when I met Ruth,' he said. 'I'd just bought my first car, an ancient old Ford with leather seats. I wanted to go over west for the weekend. It was a hot summer, and the city was killing me. I wanted to start living. I remember starting out in Dublin and not really knowing where I was headed. It could be Clare or Galway or Mayo. I turned the radio up real high. I had a picture of myself – you know those shots of young American guys driving along the Californian coast in open cars with girls beside them, playing loud music – well, that's who I wanted to be.

'Anyway, out near Maynooth, there was a girl on the road, hitching. She was holding up a piece of cardboard with Sligo written on it, and I thought, "Ah-ha, Sligo!" So I slowed down and as she was getting in I was thinking . . .

"Mmm, if she's okay, if she's nice, I'll go to Sligo, and if she's a pain I'll turn off at Kinnegad for Galway." So . . .'

'So that was Ruth and she wasn't a pain.'

He shrugged. 'That's how I met her.' He raised the glass to his lips.

'Go on,' she said. 'What happened then?'

'We drove to Sligo. She'd gotten off the boat from Holyhead that morning. She'd been working in London, and I think she'd been to France or Italy or somewhere too because she was very tanned. She was from Sligo town. She was very funny – I remember laughing a lot. On the way, she pulled out a bottle of duty-free whiskey and we started drinking it straight from the bottle. Jesus! And it was such a hot day. We got to Sligo around lunchtime, and I wanted to go out to Drumcliffe, to Yeats's grave, because I'd never been there, but she wanted to go straight to Rosses Point. She made me drive past her parents' house first so she could see it again. Like she was checking it was still there, or something. It was a tall stone house on a nice street in the town. She made me slow down, and she went really quiet as we drove by. Then after a minute or two she was happy again.

'We bought food and booze and spent the day on the beach – the far beach – at Rosses Point, lying in the sun and swimming and talking. It was one of those days where the sky is—it was the bluest I ever saw it that day. She was very young and, well . . . a dreamer. We were all dreamers in those days. I have photographs from that day somewhere – or maybe I threw them away. I called her the Hitchhiker. I'd say, "Hey, Hitchhiker, I'm hungry."'

She had seen the photographs among his things. They were mostly of the landscape, but one was of the girl. She was young and tanned and glowing. She had short dark hair and a beautiful pixie face, and she was sitting back in long grass with Ben Bulben behind her. And what must have been his shadow on the ground beside her. They must have left the beach and walked off into the fields for that photograph, she thought.

It was dark but neither of them moved to switch on a lamp. The flames of the fire had died down.

'I used to go down to her place at weekends for the rest of that summer. She played the piano, nocturnes. I didn't know what a nocturne was then. Three months after we met, we got engaged. We were just going from weekend to weekend, like two kids. She'd be upbeat and funny one weekend, and the next – so volatile, so easily inflamed. She was very bright but very fragile. Damaged. She wanted a child with me. She bit me on the face once, really hard.' He paused and brought his fingers to his cheek as if feeling for the tooth marks and she knew he was, for an instant, coming into the girl's presence again. 'The night we got engaged a crowd of us went out to a place, the Blue Lagoon, outside Sligo, and I remember thinking as we were dancing – I remember having this feeling or revelation, like those moments you read about in books – that nothing else mattered, or would ever matter again, because I'd never feel that way again.'

His voice trailed off. He got up and stood at the window. 'And for all I know she might be dead now. But even if she isn't, even if she's alive and well and walked in here this minute, I wouldn't have a word to say to her.'

She saw him again at the water's edge, with the bleached bones strewn on the sand. She remembered the empty space in the bed and the fox's eyes at dawn and the screeching gulls and the beautiful pixie face, and she thought there was something in all those things that she must fathom. She knew if she were patient, if she *fixed hard* on one image, and then the next, she would unscramble the signs and penetrate their meaning, and understanding would surely come.

'You never told me this,' she said. 'What happened?'

'She went back to England, or somewhere. I think she'd come home in the first place to get over someone, a man.'

He left the room. A *sean-nós* song drifted in from the kitchen. She pictured him standing under the light, his arms by his side, the notes and words of the song washing over him, and a face conjured, a memory resurrected, tracking him down.

They are passing through the strung-out towns west of Dublin – Enfield, Kilcock, Maynooth. Last night's name hangs in the air. The oncoming lights dazzle her. Beyond the roadside is impenetrable darkness. She has brought it on herself. She steals a glance at him, at the branded face. He has been marked by many. She closes her eyes. Was there ever one marked by her? Not many, not him.

She is suddenly cold. She cannot conceive of an end to this journey, or the tasks awaiting them at home: the switching on of lights, the unpacking, the preparation of food. She knows its end will dislodge something small and crucial and irreplaceable between them. She stirs and releases her seat belt and reaches behind for her coat. The car loses momentum abruptly, drops speed. She catches her breath. A row of red-and-white barrels signalling road repairs looms before them. Her stomach lurches. They have veered across the road into the opposite lane. Blinding white lights are coming at them. She calls out his name, harshly. His body jerks forward. 'What?' he says, in a strange ghostly voice. He had drifted to sleep. His eyes are startled, his voice the lonely dawn voice that delivers him out of sleep. He swerves and the car glances off the barrels and she cowers and covers her head, her ears. There is a streak of light on his side and the furious blare of a car horn, and then the thump and crunch of something on her side – a ditch or stones or bushes – all coming together in an instant, and then gone.

They are stopped on the hard shoulder. The lower half of the sky is amber. Cars are whizzing by on the other side. Up ahead are house lights, and beyond, the city spread out. He leans in with soft eyes and touches her arm and speaks small comforting words. She watches his mouth moving and his face and she has a sudden vision of him: his corporeal body, shrinking, contracting, growing back in time and shape – in skin and bone and hair – until he is a youth, and then a boy, and then receding further downwards and inwards until he is a plump, smiling infant and then he fades out until there is nothing left of him but a nub, and even that vanishes entirely.

And then his voice breaks through and startles her, and

he is back and whole again, and she raises her arm and opens her hand and slaps him hard and sharp on the face. And again. *Thwack*. Because something has been lost and she wants no part of him now. She wants to fling open the door and stumble into the undergrowth and crawl into a mossy place under trees and hole up there for the night.

He puts the car in gear and they move away. She is reminded of a film, and it is the final scene. A man and a woman are driving through a forest in rain, their final journey. There is no talk, no music, nothing except the constant flapping of the windscreen wipers over and back, over and back, and outside, ahead of them, shafts of sunlight filtering down through the trees, so white and blinding and terrible.

Groovejet

She wanted the lamp left on. Her hair fell over her face, and I had to keep pushing it aside to see her expression. Hers was pure selfish abandon, eyes always closed.

Don't go falling in love with me, she said.

Why? I asked. Are you dangerous or something?

We'd met in a bar called Dakota, one of those big trendy places that sprang up during the Celtic Tiger. She was with friends, and this guy was talking to her. She reminded me of Sophie Ellis-Bextor, the singer, who was in the charts at the time. Her songs keep coming into my head, even now. She laughed when I told her that – that she reminded me of the singer – and she kissed me on the cheek and said, I love you already.

The bar was crowded, and I was buzzed; the music, the atmosphere, everything about the night was intoxicating. She'd been sitting on the back of my chair when I got back from the loo.

That's my chair, I said. I didn't mean to sound so abrupt.

She stood up and looked at me. Is it, now? she said, then turned to her friends. *There's* a gentleman if ever I met one, she said, loud enough for me to hear.

I watched her after that. Wished I'd left her on the chair. I don't go out with women any more. They wreck your head so you can't eat or sleep or work.

I should've known I was on to a loser that first morning when she sent me packing at the front door.

We probably shouldn't see each other again, she said.

Why not?

Oh, you know . . .

I don't, actually.

You're too young.

I walked away with my tail between my legs. I wasn't even able to ask for her number.

But a few minutes later, before I turned off Brighton Road, I heard footsteps running behind me. I thought she'd changed her mind, but no, she felt guilty about kicking me out. Just a little.

We shouldn't see each other, she said again. In case we fall for each other.

I got rat-arsed that night.

The following Tuesday, she called my office.

See, I said, I wasn't bullshitting you about where I worked. (Actually, the first thing I said was, *Jesus, hello.*)

I hope you weren't bullshitting me about anything, she said.

I was honest, I didn't play games. I wasn't over-eager. I wasn't remote either, but I couldn't think of a thing to say to her when I was sober. Scanning my mind, scanning my mind with her scanner. Did she know how paralysed I became in her presence?

She tried to beat me at arm-wrestling, claimed she regularly beat men, and always beat women. We ran up Rathgar Road at four in the morning and this time I let her win. She wore backless sandals, and my mind went to the spot where her painted toenails gripped the sole of each sandal and held on for dear life. I thought of her face, ahead of me, all scrunched up, her shoulders taut, everything pushed into this run, and I could feel something getting away from me, and then a boldness rose up inside, an indomitable conviction to keep running and to follow her, if necessary, to the ends of the earth.

Is this your house? I asked the first night we walked up the steps of a beautiful redbrick period house.

She nodded. This is my house.

Jesus, I said.

I was twenty-three, she was thirty-seven. I told her my hero was Kofi Annan, who was Secretary General of the UN at the time. The way I gushed about him must have sounded juvenile to her. She worked in IT, she said, and was between jobs. I didn't believe her. She had books on her shelves that I didn't think were hers. Camus and Barthes, Thomas Bernhard, Schopenhauer, even Houellebecq. The nihilist's library, a bit like my own at the time. I thought they were a man's books.

Are you hiding me? I asked, one morning. Are you ashamed of me or something?

She shook her head. She was sitting across the table, smiling.

You asked me to marry you last night, she said.

I blushed, and she raised an eyebrow.

It's okay, I won't hold you to it.

She had this bowl of fruit on her table. I'd never seen such perfect apples, even stacked in those pyramids they have in posh supermarkets.

Are they real? I asked.

Are they real, she repeated.

I picked up an apple and bit into it. I thought she might wince, but she looked at me steadily as I chewed it, until we both smiled.

We always met at night. We'd drink wine and dance and later smoke my spliffs. Always mine. Oh, she paid for everything else — she had to, I was always broke by the weekend. It took nothing to get her stoned.

Don't you get lonely living all alone in this big house? I asked.

She had her feet on my lap and a cigarette in her hand. She wasn't really listening to me. She had this look — a look she often had when she was about to make some devastating observation. She exhaled slowly.

I like being alone, she said.

Don't you want a family, a husband, children? Or maybe you have them already, hidden away somewhere?

You proposing again?

In the middle of the night, I woke up and she wasn't

there. The light was on in the en suite and I lifted my head a little. She was putting pills in her mouth, and as she raised a glass of water to her lips, she caught me looking at her and pushed the door closed with her foot.

There was something about her, and about that time – and even about that house – that was unnaturally still, almost perversely still. Things looked normal; there were clothes in the wardrobe, towels in the hot press, pasta and rice in the cupboards, but from one visit to the next I had the feeling that nothing had stirred or been disturbed or even switched on – not the kettle, or the cooker, or the washing machine. As if she lived there with all those objects in some subtle body arrangement of mutual silence. Now, I'm reminded of a character in a novel I once read who had to take to his bed, so sensitive was he that he could not endure the motion of the earth. He spent his days lying down, reciting poems slowly, so that he could, at least, keep his inward gaze constant.

One night, I opened the drawer of the bedside locker and found a framed photograph of a man and a boy aged about four or five, face down under a book. There was no sign of a child's presence in the house, or a man's either. But when I woke in the morning the existence of that photograph beside my head pushed out all reasonable thoughts and words from inside me.

Why don't you eat? she'd ask when we were out for breakfast. She always had coffee and croissants, or toast lathered with butter and jam. I never got breakfast, could never face food first thing in the morning. Especially after a night with her. I felt vaguely ill, vaguely nervous all the time. But there she'd be with her wide smile, her white teeth with a spot of red lipstick, chewing her toast. How can she eat, I'd think, how can she eat at a time like this? But that's the thing. There was nothing remarkable about that time for her.

I wish I'd been braver and asked questions. But I never thought I had any right. And we only knew each other a few weeks, and she never led me to expect anything. I wasn't even sure if I was there of my own volition, or if she had somehow coaxed or seduced me into being there. There were things I chose not to see – the pristine house, the empty fridge. The medicated look in her eyes. The faint stretch marks on her belly. Once or twice she seemed to let her guard down and I thought she was on the point of telling me something. But as soon as she saw my hungry, searching eyes, she buried her face in my neck and, after a moment, pushed me away and said, way too merrily, Time to go, now.

When she called my office that Tuesday after we met and I came on the line, her first words were, Hi Kofi . . . This is Sophie. Then she laughed. I only ever called her Sophie after that. She told me I was a great kisser. I think she meant: for a young guy. She clung to me walking along city streets at night and her grip tightened when some guy got too close behind us. She pretended. I think that's how she lived – she pretended everything was fine, but she was

146

always waiting for something awful to happen. The thing is, I would have protected her, I would have watched over her day and night.

And then she just disappeared. Her phone rang out for days, and then came the three beeps indicating it had been disconnected. That was the moment I realised I was no longer free. I went round there after work and rang her doorbell. I thought of checking the hospitals, even going to the Gardaí, but who would I say I was? I found myself walking home that way after work, drawn by the warm September evenings and thoughts of summer's end. I crossed the canal with all the other workers, girls in runners, arrogant-looking guys in good suits and carrying golf umbrellas who stopped to buy milk in a corner shop and whose look – whose whole story – suddenly changed with that pint of milk. While the ducks in the canal floated by, taking no notice of anyone. Then I'd be standing in front of her house. What did I expect? That she'd appear at a window and beckon me in, or open her front door and come skipping down the steps? Or that she might, at that very moment, have to nip out to the shops for some small ingredient for the preparation of her evening meal, so that I'd be taken by surprise and have to step back and see her, secretly, from a distance. But see her, nonetheless, in the flesh, in the ordinary light of evening.

Maybe it was a brother and his son in that photograph. Maybe it was a cousin, or a friend, or the man in the moon. Just before Christmas that year, I was walking home very late one night. It was raining and the streets were like black rivers with lights reflected. There were posters up on trees and lampposts for a young man who'd gone missing after a night out a few weeks earlier. He was about my age. In the small hours of a Sunday morning, he withdrew money from an ATM machine in Baggot Street and then vanished into the night. Anyone can disappear, I thought. Then I found myself standing outside her house. It was in darkness except for the fanlight above the door. I walked up the steps and rang the doorbell, then pushed open the letterbox. The hall was just as I had remembered it, moss-green walls, a hall table, carpeted stairs leading up to the return. I pictured her bedroom, the bedside locker, the photograph in the drawer. I called out hello, and again, hello, and my voice resounded through the empty house. It came to me that she was dead, or nearly dead. I could feel my mind bending towards the truth, like a plant towards light. They were all dead, the man and the boy dead for a long time, in an accident maybe, or a drowning, or in one of those murder-suicides I read about all the time. Calm down, I told myself. Calm down, and go home, and summer will eventually come and clear your head.

Occasionally, at night, I search for her online. Her name is all I have, and it yields nothing. I surf for hours and lurk on various social media platforms. Sophie Ellis-Bextor has an active Facebook page. She's about forty now, married to a handsome musician who flies his own plane to France and back. They have a rake of kids, little red-haired boys whose faces we never see. She posts dozens of pictures – the cats, the kids, the concerts. The big lived-in kitchen. The smallest redhead sitting inside a giant plant pot. Late at night, I put 'Groovejet' on a loop and trawl back through the photos, year by year. She has a big red heart tattooed on her right arm, with the word FAMILY inside. She hasn't changed at all, she's still drop-dead gorgeous. Maybe even more so.

The Killing Line

At the very hour of my father's death, I was teaching an English Literature tutorial at my old university in Dublin. The class had started at four o'clock, and sometime between four and four-fifteen, my father sat on the edge of his hospital bed on the other side of the country to put on his socks. He had terminal cancer, and had been in hospital for tests following the completion of his chemotherapy treatment and was, now, about to be discharged. My mother went to the wardrobe to get his shoes and when she turned around he was slumped over. She said his name, Patrick, Patrick, and tried to right him, but he fell forward onto the floor. She ran out of the room, calling for help. Doctors and nurses came running; the crash cart was wheeled in, electric paddles were placed on my father's chest and everyone stood back as it jerked and bounced off the ground. Just like on TV, my mother said.

By the time I arrived, four hours later, they had removed him to the morgue for a post-mortem. My mother was in the family room with her sister and a priest. This is my son, Oliver, she said to the priest before I could embrace her. Even in times of extreme suffering, my mother places good manners and the comfort of others above all other considerations. Later, at the morgue, I was taken into a small room and left alone with my father. He was lying on a stretcher with a white sheet pulled up to his chest, his bare arms by his side. He had a mark on his forehead from the fall, and his grey hair, which was once fine and silky, was now thin and wispy from the chemotherapy. I put my hand on his arm. I used to call him Hairy Gorilla when I was small, and squeal with delight as I dared to touch his astonishingly hairy arms. When I think of those moments now, what comes to mind is something I read in the diaries of the American writer John Cheever. He was attempting to describe the love he felt for his son. What he felt, he wrote, could be accounted for biologically, as a capillary disturbance.

In the days before the hospital released my father's body back to us for the funeral, I thought of him lying in the morgue, awaiting reunion with his heart, and the heart already carved open or maybe sliced into slivers and scrutinised by strangers. I went online and sifted through images of diseased and damaged hearts, eager to find out what my father's might look like. One night I came upon photos of Albert Einstein's brain, shrunken and yellow, decades after his death. It had been stolen by Thomas Harvey, the pathologist who performed the autopsy in Princeton in 1955. Harvey sliced the brain into 240 blocks, delivered portions to researchers he liked, and then slunk off to Wichita, Kansas, with the remainder, which he kept in two Mason jars in his living room. My father would not have been enamoured of this story, or any such sensational tale.

My father was at the mart the morning I was born. He had driven my mother to the hospital late the night before. He was forty-two and she was thirty-nine. They had been married for ten years, and had probably given up hope of having a family. My father was not present at my birth. Uncertain, always, of what to do in public, his default position in a situation like this was to withdraw, disappear. I imagine he drove straight home that night, parked the car and walked around the farmyard in the dark, checking that gates and sheds and barn doors were bolted and all the animals secure, lingering in the familiar and stalling the moment when he would go inside, switch on the lights and sit there, alone, on the cusp of a new future.

I have always been aware of the outline of my father's childhood, not from anything he ever told me, but from stories his sister, Celia, and occasionally my mother, relayed. Your father was – *is* – the brightest of us all, Celia said, but you'd never know it. He was taken out of school at thirteen to farm the land when their father fell ill. His younger brothers and sisters were sent to boarding school while he worked from dawn to dusk to ensure the school fees and, later, the university fees were paid. The others went on to become teachers, bankers, civil servants, and years later when they came to visit with their own families in their good clothes and fine cars, my father maintained a shy reserve with these adult siblings that barely concealed the inadequacies he must have felt as the uneducated brother, the one left behind. I grew to recognise those moments when he guarded against shame and fell suddenly silent, afraid perhaps that his grammar or the mispronunciation of a word would betray him. He had other fears too – he was afraid of flying, and of heights, so for years it was my mother who ran up and down ladders to clean gutters or paint our farmhouse. When my mother was pregnant with me, my father climbed Croagh Patrick on Reek Sunday with my mother's two sisters and their new husbands. Certain sections of that climb are perilously steep, and my father must have been terrified on the narrow ledges near the summit. The others had not noticed him lagging behind until they heard him calling. *Wait for me*, he pleaded. *Why won't ye wait for me?* He was in an awful way, my aunt said, down on his hands and knees, nearly crying.

I used to imagine him at the mart that morning of my birth, his mind not, as usual, on the animals entering the sales ring, but anxious, distracted, momentarily veering towards hope. And then the news: a son. And the drive into Galway and the uplift – the enormous emotional uplift – he must have felt when he laid eyes on me for the first time and thought, *I made him*. In those first few years of my life, he was newly invigorated. He built gleaming new sheds, invested in the latest machinery, availed of EU grants that incentivised farmers to extend, expand, enlarge. He took me everywhere with him – to marts and agricultural shows, to ploughing championships, to buy a brand-new tractor or the latest farm machinery. He made my mother run in and get the camera and take photographs of me high up in the cab of the new tractor, or bottle-feeding Bibby, my pet lamb. He's the picture of you, Paddy, the men would tell him at the mart or outside Mass on Sunday morning. I imagine his life was lit up by such moments. I want to believe that, in those early years when he sat me on his lap on the tractor, our two heads close together, or later when we went barrelling down the road at the height of the summer's work, my existence gave him hope and confidence, and anchored him more securely in the world of men.

I had always thought I would get a premonition, some sign or visitation, when his time of death approached. But there was no tap, or draught, or down-flash of wing in class that day. We were discussing Kafka's story 'In the Penal Colony'. I have re-read and taught this story so many times that I am almost immune to its cruelty. A foreign explorer is visiting a penal colony as an observer. The officer in charge proudly shows him the apparatus used for the execution of prisoners, part of which is called the Harrow. The victim must be strapped down, naked, on a vibrating bed lined with cotton wool. A gag slots into his mouth and the Harrow is lowered mechanically over his body, and the victim's crime – whatever he has been condemned for – is inscribed on his body with long vibrating needles that pierce the skin. The Harrow shuttles back and forth and little jets of water wash away the blood into the pit underneath. When the first draft of the inscription is written on the prisoner's back, the body is turned over to provide new space for the writing. The writing goes deeper and deeper with each turning of the body. On average it takes twelve hours for the victim to die, but not before spiritual enlightenment comes to him. Enlightenment, says the officer proudly, comes even to the most dull-witted.

When I first read that story at nineteen, I discovered that Kafka, a city boy, had spent several months on a farm with his sister, Ottla, in 1917, soon after being diagnosed with tuberculosis. He chopped wood, and got to know the local farmers, and occasionally helped in the fields. I assumed it was there he encountered a harrow, which he chose as his execution tool. Years later I learned that he had written that story in 1914, before his time on the farm, but back then I was looking for affinity, reaching for any connection with Kafka, and the harrow offered a link to my own agricultural origins. There was even an old harrow, along with other obsolete farm machinery, rusting in the long grass at the end of our yard, from a time before my father concentrated solely on beef farming.

In class that day my father died, a student from Kentucky explained that a harrow is often dragged along a racetrack to level the ground before a race. Another female student expressed horror at the barbarity of the story, and astonishment at the mind of a man who could conjure up such a depraved instrument of torture. Then, as usual, the discussion turned to Kafka himself, with his sensitive soul, his poor health, his cruel father, his broken engagements. The

Kentucky girl said Kafka both attracted and repelled her. She was shocked to read that he visited prostitutes. He was unfair to the women he loved, she said, and maybe even to Hermann, his father, who simply could not comprehend his strange son.

Halfway through 'In the Penal Colony', a condemned man is stripped naked and laid under the Harrow for execution. The officer in charge, who fears this method of justice will soon be phased out, implores the explorer to speak to the new commandant in favour of its continued use. When the explorer refuses this request, things take a sudden turn. The officer frees the condemned man, strips off his own clothes, lies on the bed and takes the filthy gag into his mouth. When the Harrow is set in motion, it malfunctions, and instead of slowly inscribing the officer's skin, it jabs violently at his body. When the operation ends, the Harrow rises with the body still stuck on it, like a pig on a spit. The face of the corpse shows no sign of redemption – the officer has been denied the mystical experience, the spiritual enlightenment, that he had extolled as the benefit of this method of justice.

Just before my father started his chemotherapy treatment, I took him to a spiritual healer he'd read about in the local newspaper. Every week, crowds flocked to this man's healing sessions at a prayer centre called Damascus House at the other end of the county, and some claimed to be cured. It was May and we drove between hedgerows blooming with whitethorn and fields of fresh grass where cattle, newly released after the winter in sheds and slatted houses, grazed peacefully. As we drove, the green of the trees and bushes reminded me of journeys we took across the country to visit my aunts and uncles years ago, when my father would point to one 'fine place' after another, and remark on the size of the fields or the sheds or the grain silos, and admire the neatly clipped hedges in Meath and Kildare, and my mother and I, content to be on this mini holiday, would join him in the admiration. Now, the farms and fields we passed held nothing for him. He had long accepted that I was not coming back to farm the land, and had leased it to our neighbour, whose dairy herd crossed and recrossed the road every morning and evening at milking time, and spread out across our fields all day long.

'I think this fellow is all right,' my father said. 'Although he claims the Blessed Virgin appeared to him . . . I don't care for that sort of thing.'

'I think he's okay,' I said. 'I looked him up. The bishop gave his approval years ago, so this place is around a long time. The Church wouldn't do that if there was anything fishy or suspicious about the place.'

'No, I suppose they wouldn't . . . Or if it was any kind of cult.'

'They would not.'

He was pensive for a while. My parents were regular Mass-goers, but neither was particularly devout, and they made no objection when I stopped going in my teenage years.

'I wonder how he does it, the healing,' he said.

'I think people come up to the altar and he lays his hands on them.'

'That must be it. That article in the paper said that some people faint. If you faint, I think, that's a sign it worked.'

The prayer centre is next to the ruins of a sixth-century monastery. The modern buildings – a church with a tiled roof and a bell tower, a long low building comprising tearooms, offices and living quarters – form a cluster around a large car park. My father and I followed the other hopefuls into the church and sat in the second-row pew. In front of us was a raised altar with a crucifix and lighting candles. Organ music was playing on the sound system. I had not been in a church in a long time and I felt a stillness and peace around me. As we waited, I was suddenly overcome with a sense of sorrow for my father, and desolation for the precariousness of his life now, his immense vulnerability.

Edward Ford, a heavyset, middle-aged man who could pass as a local farmer, came out on the altar, and the crowd went silent.

'This is a spiritual hospital,' he said, 'where everyone is welcome, and where, regardless of creed or faith, we can all feel the healing power of God's love.' He had a soft voice, a kindly demeanour. 'It doesn't matter whether we're sick or well, we all need the love of Jesus.'

He read from the Gospels, preached on the urgency of repenting our sins and the need to return to God's fold. After reciting a decade of the rosary, he invited those who were ill or in need of help to write their petitions on a piece of paper and drop them in the wooden boxes near the altar.

'Have you a biro and a bit of paper?' my father whispered.

I reached into my pocket. 'Would you like me to write it for you?' I asked.

In his life, my father had had little occasion to compose personal letters or invocations like the one required now. He was silent for a few moments, then leaned in.

'Write . . . "Dear God, please cure me from this cancer."'

Later, people began to file up and stand at the altar. Edward Ford moved along the line, leaning in and speaking to each person, then laying his hands on each head and closing his eyes in prayer. My father and I watched intently. Occasionally, after the laying of hands, the person collapsed back into the arms of a relative standing behind, and the relative eased them gently onto the floor, and knelt beside them until they came round.

Finally, my father signalled to move, and we went to the altar, and I stood behind him. When Edward Ford arrived, he brought his head close to my father's and spoke into his ear, and my father spoke back, and for what seemed like several minutes the two men carried on an intense, whispered conversation. I could see their temples touching. Finally, Ford straightened up and placed his hands on my father's head and closed his eyes. I stepped closer to my father, my hands ready to catch him, and when Ford opened his eyes and made the sign of the cross over my father, my father's shoulders began to tilt backwards. I held him under his arms, but his full weight did not surrender to me, and I knew his fall was conscious, deliberate. He bent his knees, and I eased him back onto the carpet and knelt beside him. His eyes were closed, his eyelids flickering, and I sensed him praying hard, straining for a miracle.

After a while he stirred, and I led him back to our pew. We sat there for a long time, barely moving. I could feel my mind drawing closer to his, my thoughts shackled to his, lost in fear and the foreknowledge of what was to come, and I too began to pray and strain for the same miracle.

When the service ended, we rose and began to leave. For a second, relinquishing that space that had briefly enclosed and united us felt like a rupture. Outside, in the cold air, we did not know what else to do, so we followed the crowd to the tearooms. We took tea and biscuits without wanting them and stood around in our lonely, frightened state, half talking to strangers. Our eyes met, and I knew he too was wishing my mother was there; she would know what to do, how to navigate that day and steer us both back into the world again.

'I fell back, didn't I?' he said, on the way home.

'You did,' I said. 'Sure didn't I have to catch you?'

He stared out at the road ahead. 'They didn't all fall.'

I shook my head. 'No, only a few fell.'

'Was I out for long?'

'You were. A good five minutes, I'd say.'

I drove carefully to avoid bumps and potholes. He moved in his seat and took a deep breath and belched lightly.

I slowed up. 'Are you okay?'

'I feel a bit sick.'

I turned onto a side road and stopped at a gate and helped him out. He leaned on the gate and gazed out at the field. Then he bent over and vomited. I put my arm around his shoulder and held my hand to his forehead, the way my mother did when I was sick as a child. He let out a feeble moan and retched and vomited again and his body yielded against mine. A short reprieve then, before it started again. Finally, it abated, and he straightened up, and I wiped his mouth gently with a scrap of tissue.

When we set off again, he tried to pick himself up. 'Look at that fine place there,' he said, like in the old days.

'Who's this Kafka fellow?' my mother asked.

She had come into my room late one summer's evening years ago. I had finished my master's the year before and was home from Dublin for two months – helping my father on the farm by day, then spending the evening reading. I was already planning my PhD, the dissertation of which I had provisionally entitled *The Pain-Body in the Works of Franz Kafka*. I had moved some distance from the pained, angsty teenager who'd been knocked sideways by *The Metamorphosis*, but I had not yet outgrown my obsession with Kafka.

My mother's expression of interest in Kafka was her attempt at staying connected to me, and ensuring I stayed connected to her, and by extension to my father. My father never asked about my studies – too shy and out of his depth, too fearful of making an error, of saying *dessertation* instead of *dissertation*.

'He was a Czech,' I said, 'a Jew, born in Prague. He died in 1924 at age forty.'

'What happened to him?'

'TB. But he was always delicate.'

My mother picked up a volume of the Stach biography from my desk and gazed at Kafka's photo on the cover.

'He looks sad . . . And a bit odd, if you don't mind me saying so.'

I smiled. 'People did find him odd, I think.'

'I think a lot of writers are odd, aren't they?'

'Very odd, some of them!'

She flicked through the pages, looked at the photographs. She was eager to know things, find some reference or common ground.

'He was a vegetarian,' I said. 'One day he stood at an aquarium and gazed at the fish and said, "Now, finally, I can look at ye in peace, because I don't eat ye any more."'

My mother said nothing. During my teenage years I plucked the ham from my sandwiches in school and threw it to the seagulls. At home I continued to eat – or appeared to eat – meat at dinner. I'd cut it up, distribute it around the plate or slyly drop bits to the dog when my parents weren't looking. I think my mother observed this behaviour and intuited the reason. Eventually, one Sunday, when I left the meat on the plate, my father asked, 'Is that steak not done enough?', and I looked at him and said, simply, 'I can't eat meat any more.'

'His most famous story,' I continued to my mother, 'is about a young man who wakes up in bed one morning to discover he is now a giant insect.'

'Lovely.'

'In another story, there's a harrow — like a farm harrow but with sharp, vibrating needles. It's a torture machine, basically, for executing prisoners.'

She frowned and shook her head. 'I don't know why you're drawn to that kind of stuff.'

I liked having her there. I too had a longing, an old ache, to have her and my father fit into this world of books and writers and imaginative possibilities. 'Oh, something else,' I said. 'He was engaged three times. Twice to the same woman!'

'Well, I hope she had the good sense to run a mile after that.'

'Women liked him a lot, I think. He was intelligent and very sensitive. He didn't get on with his father, Hermann, at all though. Hermann was a harsh man, very overpowering and intimidating . . . Kafka had to get away from him.'

A shadow crossed her face. She left the book down. 'Sometimes, Oliver, I don't know where we got you.'

She crossed the room and stood at the door. 'You know, your father might not be perfect, and he might not be well educated, but he's no Hermann Kafka either.'

For years there was a framed photograph on top of our TV of me, aged ten, and my father, standing together with one of our prize-winning bullocks. The bullock has a red

164

rosette on his head, and my father is holding him by a rope. I am holding the prize-winner's cup and my father's hand is on my shoulder, and I am beaming. Almost every year when I was a child, we had at least one prize-winning bullock at the local agricultural show, which took place early in spring. It was the only time I was allowed a day off school, and I understood that once I started secondary school, even that privilege would end. The photograph was taken by a professional photographer and appeared in the *Connacht Tribune*. The following week, my mother drove to the newspaper's office in Galway and ordered three copies of the photograph, one of which she framed.

Every spring, my father sent up to a dozen cattle a week to the factory for slaughter, the prize-winners always the first to go. On Tuesday mornings, we would get up in the dark to separate those chosen to go from the rest of the herd. When we had them penned and ready, we'd wait in the yard until we heard the factory lorry out on the main road slow up, change gears and turn in our avenue. Soon the headlights appeared along the gable end of the house and across the roof of the barns and finally shone in our faces as the lorry pulled into the yard. Jimmy, the driver, would reverse up to the pen, lower the ramp and we'd have the cattle loaded in minutes.

'Go back to bed for another while, Oliver,' my father would say. Then he'd hop in the jeep and follow the lorry to the meat factory. My mother would make a big fry-up breakfast for herself and me, and we'd sit at the kitchen table until dawn broke and I'd have to get ready for school.

One Tuesday morning after we'd loaded the cattle, my father turned to Jimmy. 'I'm going to take this lad with me today, Jimmy, if his mother allows him off school.'

I shot a look at my mother, who was smiling.

'Take your time,' Jimmy said. 'There's a long queue down there. These lads will be in lairage for a couple of hours.'

I had never been to the meat factory before. When we passed the village of Athleague, it loomed up ahead, a massive concrete building with a corrugated-iron roof, like one of the factories in the industrial estates in Galway. Lorries and tractors and trailers queued at the entrance and others, their cargo delivered, exited. We drove in a separate entrance and parked in the car park and walked into the office building and climbed the stairs.

'Are mine gone through yet, Cathal?' my father asked at the hatch.

The man inside checked his screen. 'Not yet, Paddy. They went up the line ten minutes ago, so it won't be long.'

We walked along a corridor to the cafeteria.

'Give this lad an extra rasher, there, Clare,' my father said to the woman at the serving counter. 'It's his first visit.'

My father greeted men at nearby tables. Then a man came and stood at our table.

'Are yours killed yet, Paddy?'

'They're gone up the line,' my father said. 'We're waiting for the figures.'

'Do you ever send any to Ballyhaunis?' the man asked, and drew on his cigarette.

'The halal place. No, I never bothered.'

166

'I sent a lorryload last month . . . They slit the animals' throats, you know. It's their religion.'

'So I believe. I don't think they use stun guns at all, do they?'

'I don't think so. They're nearly all Pakistani lads working there. Pat Byron brought me up the line the day I was there. I couldn't believe it, but isn't there a fellow standing there especially to say a prayer into the bullock's ear just before he's killed. Some kind of holy man standing there all the time, saying, "Allah, Allah" or something into the bullock's ear . . . They kill sheep as well. Tuesdays for sheep, Thursday for cattle. No pigs though.'

He offered my father a cigarette. My father shook his head and reached into his pocket.

'Oliver, I must have left my pipe and tobacco in the jeep. Will you run down and get them for me?'

The lorries and tractors and trailers were still coming and going, but there was no longer a queue. I walked away from the car park towards a sign that said LAIRAGE. One end of the factory was open, and inside, reaching deep into the building, was a sea of cattle, all packed into pens. I had never seen so many — not on the busiest day at the mart. The noise was deafening; cattle lowing, engines revving, gates banging. There was no point in looking for our cattle; the man at the hatch said they were already gone up the line. I walked along by the pens. There was no sign for the line. Then I walked out into the fresh air again and around the back of the factory, where it was quieter. They were probably killed by now, I thought. I pictured them being shunted up a long passageway, which I assumed was called the line, one behind the other, or worse – getting separated in the melee. They had been together on our farm, day and night, for over two years. I came to a gate with a yellow sign: NO UNAUTHORISED ACCESS. The gate was unlocked and I went through. I walked along the edge of the building, keeping close to the high wall. At the far end I could see a big yellow skip against the wall, with markings on the side.

The skip was full of hooves, bloodied feet freshly cut off just above the dew claw. I leaned in over the top and then heard something – a rumble – and jumped back. A clatter of hooves – fifteen, maybe twenty – came tumbling down a metal chute and landed on top of the others. Then a short interval before another rush of hooves. I drew back from the edge. Their feet were in there somewhere.

I ran back the way I'd come, and brought my father's pipe and tobacco to him.

'Are you all right?' he asked, frowning, when I handed them to him.

I nodded. 'Yeah, fine.'

'Are you sure? Would you like another piece of toast – or a scone? Clare makes nice scones. Run up there and get yourself a scone and some jam.'

When I started university in Dublin, my father bought me a secondhand car to spare me the trouble of taking buses and trains, and in the hope that I would come home every weekend. And I did, at the start, arriving down late on

Friday evening, studying for a few hours on Saturday before going to town to meet old school friends. I'd help my father too, mending fences, painting gates, nothing too demanding. We did not have much to say to each other. He did not know what to ask about my college life. Before I left on Sunday afternoons, he checked the engine oil and the tyres, and my mother packed fresh bread and vegetables and occasionally – perhaps in the hope that I might be tempted – a little plastic bag with steak or lamb chops. When I got to my flat in Dublin I microwaved the meat, cut it up into small pieces and threw it to the stray cats out the back or dropped it along the canal for the seagulls on my way into town to meet friends or, later, my girlfriend Ciara.

One Sunday evening, as I was driving back to Dublin during my second year in college, a weekly documentary programme came on the radio. *Doc on One* opened with the sound of a knife being sharpened. Rob, the narrator, was recalling the year he spent working in a meat factory, and how certain songs wormed their way into his consciousness – earworms, they're called. A snippet of the song 'Bright Eyes' dropped in and then faded out. When Rob named the location of the meat factory – Athleague – my heart jumped, and I turned the volume high. He described the lorryloads of cattle arriving, the pens of Charolais, Simmental, Aberdeen Angus, the roaring of the cattle, the noise, the chaos, and I could see it all again. The animal is stunned at the start of the killing line, he said, and then hoisted up by the back leg and moved along to the blood bath. 'The animals are still sort of half alive — well, the brain is dead,' Rob said, 'but the body still has muscle memory . . . still twitching and kicking all over the place. You'd have a big eight-hundred-kilogram bullock hanging by its back leg, swinging around the place . . . You hold on to the front leg with one hand, and you drive the knife up into the throat area just above the head, then stick it right up towards the heart, giving it a twitch at the top, where you cut the jugular . . . and all the blood rushes out and down into the blood bath . . . And then you cut off the two front legs at the knee, the hock area. You're doing like six hundred cattle a day. It's savage. From seven in the morning to seven in the evening, and some days you have to switch off the brain and just go to some-where else . . . And then the line moves on, every thirty seconds, to the next station . . .'

Then a verse of 'Starry, Starry Night' faded in and out.

Rob worked mostly at the flanking station, where he stood on a steel platform with pedals which, when tapped, raised and lowered the platform. High up, six feet in the air, he'd stick the knife into the skin above the testicles and he'd tap the pedal and the platform would shoot down, and as he descended he'd slice open the skin right down to the chest, his knife running through it like butter. Then he'd hit the pedal and zip back up again and pull away the skin, ripping it off all the way down until the stomach was bare and the yellow fat was exposed and the steam was rising off the flayed bullock. And then, beep-beep, the bullock moved on and the next one arrived.

* * *

That night, in my flat in Dublin, I opened my laptop and typed in 'meat factory killing line'. Images flooded my screen. A necklace of pig carcasses, sawed open frontally and hanging in a line, looking like they were all holding hands. A terrified cow upended in a mechanical killing box. Rows of just slaughtered cattle hanging on hooks by the back leg, their heads intact, their eyes open, their tongues out, their hides half peeled off.

I went down the rabbit hole that night. I learned the language of slaughter, the means of evisceration. I saw how some companies – the French and the Americans especially – appear less cautious, or less ashamed, about revealing the practices of the killing line, or about advertising slaughter-line equipment. Breast-openers, hide-skinners, rib-removers, udder-removers. A myriad of instruments. Pig-flappers 'for the efficient goading and prodding of animals, help reduce the risk of blood splash and death from heart attacks'. Rob had not mentioned these. Or the practice of rodding – inserting a rod into the neck of the animal at slaughter and drawing out the oesophagus, detaching it from the stomach and then clamping it – which 'significantly reduces the risk of burst bellies'.

It must have been after midnight when I came on the plugs. Frontal head plugs. Flange plugs. Bung plugs. There is no end to the indignities. Bung closure: the closing-off of the rectum by cutting around the anus, placing a bag over the rectum and securing it in place with an elastic band.

I got up and walked around the flat and sat down again. I could not stop. If I stopped, I would not go back, and then I would never know. I lost track of time, and feeling. I went from site to site, reading eyewitness accounts from factories and backstreet abattoirs, watching films by under-cover activists. Young men from Europe, America, Brazil, their faces pixelated.

> 'Bringing [cows] around the corner and they get stuck up in the doorway, just pull them till their hide be ripped . . . Breaking their legs . . . And the cow be crying with its tongue stuck out. They pull him till his neck just pop.'

> 'Hogs get stressed out pretty easy. If you prod them too much, they have heart attacks. If you get a hog in the chute that's had the shit prodded out of him and has a heart attack or refuses to move, you take a meat hook and hook it into his bunghole. You try to do this by clipping the hipbone. Then you drag him backwards. You're dragging these hogs alive, and a lot of times the meat hook rips out of the bunghole. I've seen hams — thighs — completely ripped open. I've also seen intestines come out. If the hog collapses near the front of the chute, you shove the meat hook into his cheek and drag him forward.'

Dawn was breaking when I moved the cursor to close the tabs. Ads began to pop up at the side of the screen. Chainmail Aprons and Tunics, from €305. Clip Air 800T Double Hook Rodder, €187. *Lamb plugs, €49 for 2,000.* At the sight of those words — the co-positioning of those two words – I could feel a division occurring within myself. I could see Bibby. I could hear her, in a sea of lambs. I closed the laptop and stared at the wall. In the bathroom I switched on the light and stood at the mirror, and for the first time I understood how a person could hurt themselves, or hurt others.

'Could you not get a teaching job around here?' my father asked me one weekend. I was thirty then, and had just accepted a temporary teaching job at the university in Dublin. 'Or a job lecturing in the university in Galway? I thought that's why you did the PhD.'

'It was. But there aren't any vacancies in my subjects.'

'So Dublin is the only place you can get a job, is it? After all the years of studying?'

My heart was pounding. He had never spoken to me like this.

'Something might come up down the line,' my mother said. 'You never know, in a year or two, something might open up in Galway.'

Later, when my father had gone up to bed, she flashed me a rare look of annoyance.

'Do you know what it took for him to ask that question?'

I nodded.

'He never thought it would come to this. God knows, he never expected you to farm *full-time*. He always wanted you to have a university education and a good job.' Her face had a look of pleading. 'You could do it part-time, even as a hobby, Oliver.'

I shook my head.

'You wouldn't have to lift a finger. He'd manage it for you. The farm has never been in better shape – he has it all organised in a such a way that there's very little labour involved any more.'

'Please, Mam, I can't.'

'It was my hope, too, that you'd get a job and settle down close to home. That time when you were going out with that girl Ciara, I thought maybe . . . She was a lovely girl, a bright girl.'

The relationship with Ciara had fizzled out after eight or nine months. Towards the end, before either of us was brave enough to call time, I made the mistake of taking her down west one weekend.

'Do you ever hear from her?'

'She went to Australia a few years ago. She's teaching over there, the last I heard.'

'You could still come back, Oliver. Build a house on the land, like other young fellows around.'

'I'm sorry.'

I had never had the conversation with my father, never told him straight out that I could not look into their eyes every day. In my *mind* I had argued with him, and harangued him. *Don't you see how cruel it is? How innocent they are? They're entirely at our mercy. And you don't even know the harm it might be doing to yourself! Don't tell me it doesn't affect you. You feed them and care for them day in, day out, for years. They trust you . . . And then you load them up and deliver them to their killers. What's that doing to your own psyche, Daddy, your own soul?* I said none of

174

it, but he knew anyway, because somehow these things are transmitted.

My mother looked out at the dark.

'You read all these books, Oliver,' she said, quietly, 'and you get all those degrees . . . And you have a nice clean job and lovely white hands – look at your beautiful hands! But don't forget you were reared and educated on the fat of the land – on the backs of animals.' Her voice began to break. 'All his life your father made sacrifices for others – he put his own brothers and sisters through college, and then he did the same for you. And he was happy to do that, and proud of you! But then you reject everything he stands for.'

After that long night, years ago, when I stayed up reading the factory workers' testimonials, I could not get out of bed for days. I felt doomed, that nothing I did would ever have meaning again. One morning when I switched on my phone, I had twenty-three missed calls from my mother. Before I got around to calling her back, she appeared at my flat door, having driven to Dublin alone. She asked no questions, but took me home and nursed me through the next few months until that fissure closed, and I could look out one morning in February at a ferocious storm that battered the trees outside my bedroom window. I watched the crows' nests high up in the bare branches being pitched about in the gale-force winds, and marvelled that they could hold, that their construction from twigs and moss and feathers could survive such elemental forces, while the crows themselves hunkered down inside as hailstones pelted down on their heads.

'You're a good man, Oliver,' she said now, 'a *kind* man, I know you are. You feel for people and animals alike. So how is it that you have so little feeling for your own father?'

My father died from sudden cardiac arrest caused by an electrical malfunction which prevented his heart from pumping blood to his brain, his lungs and other organs. He would have lost consciousness immediately, and died within minutes. A few months later, taking us through the post-mortem report, his GP cited Long QT syndrome, a condition that often goes undetected, as the likely culprit. A Long QT syndrome episode or interval can, I read, be triggered by everyday events such as being startled by a noise, or experiencing intense emotions such as fear, or anger, or pain.

I stayed home with my mother the summer after his death. She had a great need to talk about my father. She recounted over and over the details of the day he died – the fall off the bed, the pandemonium that ensued. 'Did I tell you I said an Act of Contrition in his ear when he was on the ground?' she asked. She fretted over whether he had concealed his heart trouble from us, or if it had been missed because of the cancer, or if she herself had neglected him. One morning she said, 'I had a terrible dream last night, that the hospital had forgotten to put your father's heart back inside his body. It was night-time and I was at his grave, digging secretly in the dark, trying to get to the coffin and put it back inside him.'

Over time, the worst of the grief has eased. My father

had a full life, I tell myself, and a swift death. Sitting at my desk late at night, I remember the long car journeys of my childhood, the tractor rides on summer evenings, his hand on my shoulder at the agricultural show. I remember the trip to the healing centre that May day, and his intense whispered conversation with the healer, and how that journey had briefly reconciled and returned us to each other. And then I remember my mother, alone in her kitchen on the other side of the country, and I think how she was always the bridge between my father and me, how she is still the bridge.

I do not know if my father ever gave consideration to the life of a bullock or any animal, to its moment-by-moment existence, or the intimate reality of its death. And even if he had, he would not have dwelt on it for long. Still, I would like to have talked to him about this, and other things. I would like to have told him what I think. But how could I tell him that somewhere along the way, something must have happened to me that altered me biologically – a shock maybe, a child's version of a Long QT syndrome interval? Or tell him that if another son – a different child – had been conceived and born to him and my mother, if a different sperm had penetrated a different ovum, that other child might never have wandered around the back of a meat factory when he was ten and found a skipful of hooves; that other child might not have grown into a man who is so obsessed with instruments of torture and the minds that conjure them that he cannot see the word 'plug' without caving in, and who secretly prays that reciting the Shahada into the ear of a terrified animal will bring comfort to the animal in his hour of death? How could I tell my father that he and my mother might have been better off remaining childless, or that I might have been better off not being born, or, at least, not being born to them?